ROMANCE RIDES THE RIVER

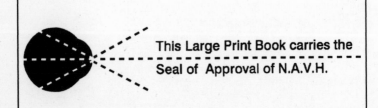

This Large Print Book carries the
Seal of Approval of N.A.V.H.

ROMANCE RIDES
THE RIVER

COLLEEN L. REECE

THORNDIKE PRESS
A part of Gale, Cengage Learning

GALE
CENGAGE Learning·

Detroit • New York • San Francisco • New Haven, Conn • Waterville, Maine • London

GALE
CENGAGE Learning®

Copyright © 2010 by Colleen L. Reece.
California Brides Series #2.
All scripture quotations are taken from the King James Version of the Bible.
Thorndike Press, a part of Gale, Cengage Learning.

Thorndike Press® Large Print Clean Reads.
The text of this Large Print edition is unabridged.
Other aspects of the book may vary from the original edition.
Set in 16 pt. Plantin.

LIBRARY OF CONGRESS CATALOGING-IN-PUBLICATION DATA

Reece, Colleen L.
    Romance rides the river / by Colleen L. Reece. — Large print edition.
        pages ; cm. — (Thorndike Press large print clean reads) (California brides series ; #2)
    ISBN-13: 978-1-4104-6170-4 (hardcover)
    ISBN-10: 1-4104-6170-X (hardcover)
    1. Large type books. I. Title.
PS3568.E3646R665 2013
813'.54—dc23   2013020738

Published in 2013 by arrangement with Barbour Publishing, Inc.

Printed in the United States of America
1 2 3 4 5 6 7 17 16 15 14 13

For Susan K. Marlow, research expert
and editor extraordinaire.

ONE

June 1880
San Joaquin Valley, California
"I'm not going to school in Madera any longer."

Dolores Sterling's personal Declaration of Independence hit the spacious kitchen of the white stucco, Spanish-style ranch house on the Diamond S cattle ranch like a burst of gunfire.

Solita, the diminutive Mexican housekeeper, dropped the tortilla she had been tossing. Dori's brother, Matt, straightened from lounging in the doorway. Storm signals flashed in his bright blue eyes, eyes the same color as his sister's. He parked his hands on his hips and glared down at her. Four inches taller than Dori's five-foot-seven height, Matt's high-heeled cowboy boots allowed him to tower even farther over her.

"You what?"

Dori gave Matt her most charming smile.

"I'm going to Boston for a three-year term." She clenched her hands behind her back and tossed her head until her black curls danced. "I already wrote to the school. They are holding a place for me. All you have to do is to send the money."

Matt snorted. "I do, do I? What if I refuse?"

"Then you'll cause me to break my word. I told them I was coming." Dori ignored Solita's gasp. "It's a matter of honor, Matt."

"What's honorable about going behind my back and promising such an outlandish thing?" he raged.

If Dori hadn't known how much her brother — who had taken their father's place after he died — doted on her, she'd have been intimidated. She mumbled, "Sorry, but I figured you'd say I'm too young. I'm not. I'll be sixteen years old in a few months. You need to start treating me like a young lady, not a little girl."

Matt exploded with laughter. "You, a young lady?" He pointed at her worn riding skirt and vest. "How do you think you will stack up against those Boston blue bloods?"

Dori proudly raised her head. "I'd rather have good, red, western blood than all the blue blood in America," she retorted. "Besides, I can become just as much a lady as any sissy East Coast girl." She ignored the cynical little voice inside that challenged, *oh yeah?* and rushed on. "This is where I'm going." She held out a worn magazine advertisement extolling the virtues of Brookside Finishing School for Young Ladies in Boston, Massachusetts.

Matthew said nothing.

Dori turned to Solita. "*You* think I should go, don't you, Solita?"

The housekeeper, who had become Matt and Dori's substitute mother after the death of Rebecca Sterling many years before, waited until Matt finished reading the advertisement. Then she quietly said, "*Señor* Mateo, I think that *Señora* Sterling would be glad for her daughter to attend such a school."

"*Gracias, gracias,* Solita." Dori grabbed the housekeeper. She whirled her into a mad dance, blew Matt a kiss, and dashed out of the kitchen. With Solita on her side, Matt would never refuse to let her go — or would he? Not quite certain, Dori paused just outside the doorway. She knew eavesdropping was wrong, but her whole future hung in the balance.

"Our *casa* will seem empty, but you must release the *señorita,*" Solita said. "She is unhappy here, like a little bird wanting to try her wings and fly. Your *mamá* and *papá* would have allowed it, had they lived. Since they are no longer with us, you must decide what is best for her, not what is best for you." She sighed. "And for me."

Dori sneaked away, knowing she had won.

Once Matt reluctantly consented, the next few weeks flew by in a maze of preparations. Matt paid the exorbitant fee required by Miss Genevieve Brookings, owner and headmistress of the Brookside School. He imported a dressmaker from Fresno. If Dori was going back east, she would go in style with the proper clothing.

Unfortunately, Dori's idea of "proper clothing" did not coincide with Miss Mix's. When the prim dressmaker produced a pair of corsets, Dori rebelled. "I don't wear corsets. My brother thinks it's unhealthy for young girls to be forced into instruments of torture for the sake of fashion."

Miss Mix gasped. "You discuss ladies' undergarments with your *brother*?"

Dori reveled in the woman's horror. "Of course," she said innocently. "He's so much older than I that he helped dress me when I was a little girl."

Disapproval oozed out between the pins in Miss Mix's pinched mouth for the remainder of the dressmaking sessions, and she reminded Dori that "Pride goeth before a fall."

Dori came off triumphant by correctly quoting Proverbs 16:18: " 'Pride goeth before *destruction*, and an haughty spirit before a fall.' " When Dori's trunks were packed and ready for the long train trip, they contained both lovely and practical clothing: hats, gowns, shoes, etc. — but nary a hated corset.

Dori enjoyed the train ride back east with Matt, despite being cooped up in a small space. When she grew weary of sitting in the plush seats, she strolled through the cars, wondering. Where were her fellow passengers headed? Dori smiled to herself. Surely no one else was going to the Brookside School. The knowledge made her feel superior. So did dreaming about what Madera would think of her when she finished her schooling. *I'll come home a young woman,* she realized. *The cowboys on the Diamond S will gape — but my girlhood will be left behind. Will becoming a lady mean giving up the freedom I've always enjoyed?*

Like a summer squall that attacks the unwary without warning, a new and unwelcome thought plagued Dori. She had shrugged off Matt and Solita's warnings that some of the young ladies at Brookside might look down on her. Who cared? She could hold her own against any snobbish girl. *But what if I meet and fall in love with an easterner? Someone who considers everything west of Chicago uncivilized? Could I give up my home for him?* Dori sniffed. *Lord, it was fine for Ruth in the Bible to promise she'd follow her mother-in-law wherever Naomi led, but I'm no Ruth.*

Dori squirmed in her seat. How foolish to be concerned over what might lie ahead. A scripture Solita often quoted when Dori or Matt worried about what might happen came to mind. *"Take therefore no thought for the morrow: for the morrow shall take thought for the things of itself. Sufficient unto the day is the evil thereof."*

It was enough for now that each day brought new sights — the wonder of America. Dori had never been farther from Madera than Fresno, and a visit to San Francisco several years earlier. She shivered. The tall buildings huddled together for protection against the Pacific Ocean on one side and San Francisco Bay on the other had seemed to close in on her. Dori had never seen so much water, not even when the rivers around Madera flooded. She'd sighed with relief when she and Matt left the city behind.

Dori found Chicago even more crowded and stifling than San Francisco. Changing trains swept away her feelings of superiority. Big and bustling, with people rushing to and fro in and out of the station's doors, Dori felt dwarfed by its immensity. She stayed close to Matt until her personal needs could no longer be denied. A smiling agent directed her to the proper place.

"Don't be too long," Matt warned. "Our train was late so we only have a short layover here."

"All right." Heart pounding, Dori took careful note of the way to the facility so she would know how to get back to Matt. She had no trouble reaching the room marked LADIES and hurriedly took care of her needs. She washed her hands at one of the gleaming sinks and started back toward Matt, but was caught up in a horde of people rushing in the opposite direction. All of them appeared to know exactly where they were going. Feeling like she'd been trapped in a stampede, Dori became hopelessly disoriented. She couldn't see over the tall hats many of the gentlemen wore. Was this how a salmon felt while trying to swim upstream? For the first time in her life, Dori panicked. Where was Matt? What should she do? What if they missed their train?

She swallowed hard. *Please, God, help me find my brother.*

It was the first prayer Dori had uttered in weeks, except for asking God to make Matt let her attend Brookside School. Fear threatened to suffocate her. What if God didn't answer? The crowd of pushing, shoving people swept her along. Caught in their midst, Dori screamed at the top of her lungs, "Matt! Where are you?"

Her cry for help was lost in the clamor. A train whistle shrieked a warning, summoning passengers to get on board or be left behind. The multitude reached the outside doors, Dori still in their midst. If she couldn't free herself, she would be carried onto the train with Matt left behind. Or — Dori blanched — forced onto the wrong train.

Terror changed her to a wildcat. Elbows out, Dori rammed into those around her. "Get out of my way!" she shouted. Muttered curses from those she struck rang in her ears, but she cleared a passage and fought her way to the side. She clung to a doorpost while the uncaring crowd rushed on.

The wheels of the train began to move.

14

Dori screamed for her brother again. A heavy hand fell on her shoulder. Tears streaming, she looked up. "Matt! Thank God." Dori sagged in his arms.

Matt snatched her up and raced toward the already-moving eastbound train.

"Hurry," the conductor cried from his position at the bottom of the steps.

With a mighty leap Matt reached the bottom step and lunged up to safety. The conductor followed and raised the steps behind him.

All Dori could do was cling to her brother and cry.

The *clackety-clack* of the incoming train's wheels dwindled into silence. Brakes screeched. The engine shuddered, gasped, and died — as if glad to have reached its destination. It had been a long, hard run from Madera, California, to Boston, Massachusetts: three thousand miles of mountains and canyons, cities and small settlements, and always that monotonous *clackety-clack* of gigantic wheels carrying Dolores Sterling away from everything she knew.

"Well, we're here." Matt stepped into the aisle and stretched. "Need a hand?"

Dori shook her head, not trusting herself

to speak. What she could see of Boston through the train's dirty windows depressed her. The drizzle from the weeping skies added to her misery. So did the tall buildings closing in on each side of the street and threatening to smother her.

Dori shuddered and pulled her traveling cloak closer around her trembling body. She clutched her reticule and followed Matt up the aisle and onto the station platform. Once inside the horse-drawn carriage that rumbled and swayed over the cobblestone street, she huddled in the corner of the musty-smelling vehicle, closed her eyes, and gulped back homesickness. *I can't look back.* Yet she couldn't help reliving the frightening incident in the Chicago train station.

A hard jolt flung Dori against Matt. She opened her eyes. She was no longer lost and terrified in the Chicago station. Or on the train, badly shaken and unable to tell Matt what had happened and how frightened she'd been. She was in Boston with a single, unanswerable question drumming in her brain: *Why did I plead, beg, and insist on coming east to school instead of staying home on the Diamond S where I belong?*

Two

The creaking carriage stopped in front of an ivy-covered building that jutted three stories into the scowling sky. Dori stared at the fancy sign identifying it as the Brookside Finishing School for Young Ladies. Several smaller attached buildings trailed away from the main structure like the tail of a kite. This gloomy place couldn't be the academy Dori had seen advertised. Enticed by glowing descriptions of sunlight sifting through huge trees and dappling the manicured lawn, she'd dreamed about drinking lemonade there. Or — better yet — beating a bevy of well-dressed young ladies at croquet. Now the only sign of life in the sodden front yard was a pair of long, skinny legs beneath a black umbrella.

Matt paid the driver and held out his hand to assist Dori.

"Step lively, miss," the driver advised. "Looks like it's going to pour."

Stepping lively was the last thing Dori wanted to do, but Matt helped her out of the carriage and hurried her along a cobblestone walk. Before he could lift the heavy knocker, the massive doors swung open. A cadaverous-looking individual with an expression as mournful as his night-black clothing bowed. "Come in, sir, miss. I'm Scraggs. May I take your coats?"

Dori stared. This caricature of a man who looked like he'd stepped out of a Charles Dickens novel must be a butler. How Curly and Bud and Slim would howl if they could see her now. A ripple of laughter escaped.

Matt sent her a disapproving glance but Scraggs didn't even blink. He efficiently hung their wet garments on a nearby rack and said in a voice as colorless as his long face, "This way, please. Miss Brookings is in her office."

He even talks like a Dickens character, Dori thought. *If he ever smiles, I'll wager his face would crack.* She followed Matt and Scraggs down the hall that appeared longer than the main street in Madera. Their footsteps sounded loud on the marble floor and echoed from the high ceiling and cream-colored walls adorned with a frieze of smirking cupids. How different from the Diamond S ranch house and its colorful

18

Spanish-style decor. No wonder Scraggs looked like he never smiled. Who *could* smile in this morgue watched over by those awful cupids?

When they reached a door marked OF-FICE, Scraggs tapped.

"Enter."

The chill in the word sent shivers down Dori's spine.

Scraggs swung the door open and announced, "Mr. Sterling. Miss Sterling." He waited for Matt and Dori to go in, then stepped out and closed the door behind him.

Dori's heart fell like a rock with her first glimpse of Miss Genevieve Brookings, owner and headmistress of the Brookside School. Worse, Dori's besetting sin flared. Solita had warned her since childhood about the danger of relying on first impressions, but Dori continued to make them. Now, inwardly rebelling about her intolerable situation, she curtseyed when presented, then sank into a hard chair. She looked at the skeleton-thin, pale-faced headmistress with flaming red hair seated behind a huge desk and decided she detested her. Especially when the middle-aged woman in stark black silk turned to Matt, who occupied the chair next to Dori.

"*Dear* Mr. Sterling," Miss Brookings gushed, "we are *so* pleased that you chose our school for your charming sister. I am sure she will be a credit to Brookside. We cater to only the finest young ladies."

Dori's lip curled. *She should be called Babbling Brook. She runs on and on like the creeks in the Sierra Nevada.* Dori bit her lip to keep from disgracing herself by laughing.

"We *do* have a slight problem." Miss Brookings's thin hands twisted a white handkerchief. "I, however, am sure it can be worked out to everyone's satisfaction. As you know, we limit our enrollment to twenty young ladies. When we accepted Dolores, we didn't realize Gretchen van Dyke would be returning this year. She is the only child of one of our wealthiest merchants and has been with us since she was twelve. Unfortunately, the poor girl fell ill last spring and was forced to leave school. I'm happy to say she has now regained her health and is eager to return."

She bared her teeth in a travesty of a smile. "I apologize for not informing you of this earlier. By the time we realized Gretchen was returning to school, you were already on your way." She spread her hands in a helpless gesture. "We can't afford to offend dear Mr. van Dyke, now can we?"

Joy exploded in Dori like fireworks on the Fourth of July. Bless Gretchen, the merchant's daughter. Dori tingled with anticipation until she could barely sit still. Her heart raced. She felt her mouth widen into a delighted grin. Thanks to "dear Mr. van Dyke's only child," Dori Sterling could go home without losing face.

Yippee-ki-ay!

She clapped one hand over her mouth, fearing she had spoken aloud.

Matt stared at Miss Brookings. His words fell like ice pellets into the silence. "Madam, we paid your fee in good faith. This van Dyke girl will not be taking my sister's place." He stood, as if to end the conversation. "Now if you will excuse me, I have a train to catch."

Dori felt her heart break from disappointment. In a matter of seconds, she had plunged from the heights of happiness to the depths of despair. She stood, tried twice to speak, and at last got a few words out. "M–Matt," she stammered, "if the other girl really wants to come back, I . . ."

Her brother's jaw set in a way that boded no good for Miss Brookings, who had sprung from her chair and come around from behind the desk. "You are staying, Dori, or I'll see that the authorities hear of this." He took Dori's arm. "Walk me to the door."

Miss Brookings's pale eyes filled with alarm. *So she's human, after all,* Dori thought. *Or maybe afraid of what Matt might do. A lot of good that will do me. The Babbling Brook will hate me for sure if Matt makes her let me stay.*

"Please, Mr. Sterling, you misunderstand me." Miss Brookings's crumpled handkerchief fell to the carpet. "I am making an exception to accommodate your sister. Dear Gretchen is just your age, Dolores. You'll be in the same grade. But" — she shook her head — "you'll have to work hard to keep up with her. Gretchen is our finest student." She paused, then added, "I just know that you two will become bosom friends."

Dori ducked her head to hide a grin. Had the prim and proper headmistress really said *bosom* in front of Matt? Become friends with the van Dyke girl? Dori would sooner get bucked off a wild mustang. The Babbling Brook rushed on.

"The only thing is, she will have a roommate instead of occupying the private room you requested. Miss van Dyke has always occupied that particular room and —"

"And now it will be necessary for her to be assigned elsewhere," Matt cut in.

22

Miss Brookings looked as appalled as Dori felt. "But, *dear* Mr. Sterling, Mr. van Dyke is our strongest financial supporter."

Matt's eyes flashed. "I don't care if he is Governor John Davis Long. I paid for a private room for Dolores, and I expect her to have it." He glared at the distraught woman. "And it had better not be some cobbled-up makeshift."

"I am sure it shall be as you say." But the venomous look she gave Dori when Matt turned toward the door warned the reluctant new addition to Brookside Finishing School for Young Ladies: Dori already had an enemy.

THREE

Hope for delivery from Dori's troubles fell to the marble floor when she took Matt's arm and traversed the long hall to the forbidding front doors. Ignoring Scraggs, who hovered nearby like an unwelcome wraith, Matt hugged her.

He looked troubled. "If the scene with Miss Brookings has made you feel unwelcome, there's still time to change your mind. There must be other schools, although it may be too late to get you in this term."

Matt's offer shone like a rainbow after rain. Dori hid her face against his shoulder. Every beat of her heart urged her to go home — but it was too late. She had teased to come. Matt had paid an exorbitant price for her tuition. With Miss Brookings so upset, Dori knew not one penny of the fee would be refunded.

The Sterling pride that had built the

Diamond S from a small spread into one of the largest cattle ranches in the San Joaquin Valley meant Dori must stay if it killed her — *and it may,* she silently added.

Dori straightened her shoulders and summoned every ounce of the acting ability she had developed over the years to get her own way. *I must give a performance worthy of Sarah Bernhardt. A performance so convincing Matt will go home believing I'm exactly where I want to be. And I must do it without lying.* She took a deep breath, mustered a smile, and looked into her brother's face.

"Don't be silly," she said, hoping the tears that welled behind her eyes would produce a sparkle but not fall and betray her. "When have you ever known me to cut and run when there was rough water? Besides," she quickly added, "I intend to hold my own against 'dear Mr. van Dyke's daughter.' "

The relief in Matt's laugh showed Dori how well she was succeeding in her role of delighted student. He hugged her and dropped a kiss on her forehead. His blue eyes so like hers darkened. "Besides, you outrank Miss Gretchen van Dyke."

"I do?" Dori gaped at him.

"Yes, my dear sister," Matt quietly told her. "She has a wealthy merchant for a father, but you are a child of the King of

25

heaven and earth."

Scraggs coughed.

Dori freed herself and whirled toward him. Was that actually approval she saw in his faded eyes?

The butler cleared his throat. "Ahem. If I may be so bold, sir, I'll be happy to look after Miss Sterling as much as my duties allow."

Remorse swept through Dori. She had unjustly categorized the butler as dour and without feelings. Now she saw kindness in his worn face — kindness that melted a bit of the ice surrounding her heart at the thought of Matt leaving without her.

Matt must have read her thoughts. He thanked Scraggs, shook his hand, then pulled Dori to him and whispered in her ear, "Remember what God told Samuel: 'The Lord seeth not as man seeth; for man looketh on the outward appearance, but the Lord looketh on the heart.' Who knows? Maybe even Miss Brookings has hidden depths." With a grin and a final hug, he stepped out into the rain, leaving Dori and the butler alone in the great hall.

"I'll have someone show you to your room," Scraggs said. "You will find a list of rules posted on the door. You need to memorize them."

A look of understanding crossed between them, making Dori feel she wasn't entirely friendless in this strange, new world.

The maid Scraggs summoned, who looked to be about Dori's age, smiled and announced, "I'm Janey." She took Dori to a corner back bedroom on the second floor. Although smaller than Dori's room at home, it was still spacious and attractively furnished. The single bed wore a damask spread that matched the draperies at two large windows. A study desk, two lamps, an ornately carved wall mirror, a comfortable-looking chair, a chest of drawers holding a porcelain bowl and water-filled pitcher, and a large wardrobe completed the ensemble.

Janey wrinkled her freckled, upturned nose. Mischief flashed in her eyes. "Miss Gretchen's going to throw a catfit when she finds out you have this room. It's the best in the school." She made a face. "Don't pay that one any mind. She's just used to having her own way." Janey began lifting gowns from Dori's trunk and hanging them in the wardrobe. "Ooh, how pretty." When she finished, she said, "You'd better change your clothes for dinner, miss." A bell chimed. "That's the first bell. The second means hurry." She gave Dori a friendly grin and vanished into the hall.

Dinner? Oh yes, eastern folk called *dinner* "lunch" and *supper* "dinner." Dori removed her traveling clothes, sponged her face and neck, and slipped into her finest gown. The rich, white silk was the epitome of elegance yet gave Dori the freedom of movement she insisted on. Miss Mix had boasted, "It's the very latest fashion. Wear it the first night, so you can make a lasting impression," she advised. "In it, you can hold your own against the finest there."

Dori caught up a gorgeous shawl Solita had made for her in Mexico's national colors: scarlet, emerald, and white. Before leaving her room, Dori paused to read the posted rules. "Ugh. There are enough rules here to choke the biggest work horse on the Diamond S." She grimaced. "God only gave the Ten Commandments. If Brookside listed all these in their advertisements, no one would ever enroll."

Among other things, Brookside young ladies were forbidden to eat in their rooms, walk beyond the school property unless accompanied by a teacher, run in the halls, or be out of their rooms after lights out. They were warned that talking, laughing, note writing, conversation by signs, eating, and leaving of seats were forbidden during study and recitation hours. Loud talking and

28

romping were prohibited. For every perfect lesson scholars received four good marks. Two entire failures in answering or general imperfect answers incurred a forfeit mark, whatever that was.

And the young ladies must never, ever be late for meals.

"I might as well be in jail," Dori muttered. She quickly read the final rule: "The Bible is the great rule of duty for both teachers and scholars. Truth and virtue, Christian kindness and courtesy, will be the governing principle of conduct to all the members of this school."

Dori raised a disbelieving eyebrow. "Teachers and scholars? I wonder if the Babbling Brook ever reads her own rules."

A second bell sent Dori scrambling to the wall mirror for a last reassuring glance, in spite of Janey's warning that it meant hurry. The white gown and brilliant shawl set off Dori's dark curls and blue eyes to perfection. She blew the looking-glass girl a satisfied smile, sailed out her door, and lightly tripped down the stairs. She followed the sound of voices and stopped in the doorway of the large dining room. Light from two chandeliers sparkled on gleaming silver and dishes. The aroma of good food lured. Suddenly hungry and fully prepared to dazzle

the Boston blue bloods with the dress Miss
Mix had predicted would "make a lasting
impression," Dori stepped inside.

FOUR

Dori entered the dining room and stopped short.

She had wanted to show the girls at Brookside Finishing School for Young Ladies that living in the West didn't mean being a barbarian. Instead, she wished she could sink through the floor.

She was the only girl in the room wearing a fancy gown.

The others wore long-sleeved grey dresses with voluminous white pinafores, identical to the school uniforms hanging in Dori's wardrobe. And the girls were staring at her with open mouths and scornful eyes.

In the pool of silence that followed Dori's grand entrance, Miss Mix's warning flashed into her mind. Pride *did* go before destruction, and mighty was the fall of Dori's haughty spirit.

"Miss Sterling, you are late," Miss Brookings snapped from her place at the head table. Triumph dripped from every word. "If you hadn't wasted time decking yourself out as if you were going to a fancy dress ball" — she cast a disparaging look at Dori's shawl — "or a costume ball, you wouldn't be tardy."

Titters ran through the room.

Humiliated but undefeated, Dori refused to take the Babbling Brook's belittling comment meekly. She quelled the roomful of giggling girls with a lightning glance, turned to the headmistress, and put on her most injured expression. "Why, Miss Brookings, I took for granted that since this is Boston, proper etiquette required me to dress for dinner. When in Rome, do as the Romans do, right?"

The headmistress's face reddened. "This is not Rome. Our young ladies only wear such garments on special occasions." She pointed to an empty chair at a nearby table where seven girls sat staring. "Take your place."

Inwardly seething, Dori obeyed. She bowed her head while Miss Brookings mumbled a boring blessing. What good was it to win the first skirmish? Dozens of hard battles lay ahead, and what chance did she have of winning the war? A quick survey of the girls around her in their regulation

uniforms left Dori unimpressed. Not [...]
looked like she had enough spunk to [...]
boo to a goose.

After introducing themselves, the gi[...]
ignored Dori until one smirking brunett[...]
spoke up. "You're the girl who stole Gretchen van Dyke's room, aren't you?"

Dori felt hot color spring to her cheeks. "I
have the room my brother paid for."

"Gretchen won't like it," Harriet sneered.
"Neither will her father."

Dori resisted the temptation to blurt out
that Gretchen and her father could go hang.
Instead, she daintily raised one shoulder
and met Harriet's unfriendly gaze head-on.
"The room is mine now." She smiled
sweetly. "Perhaps Miss van Dyke can room
with you. If you like, I'll speak to Miss
Brookings about it."

Harriet choked, gulped water from her
crystal goblet, and retorted, "We'll see about
that." Her eyes smoldered.

Appetite gone, Dori choked down what
was put before her, but only for the sake of
appearance. She'd eat dirt before letting this
pack of snobs see how upset she was. When
Miss Brookings dismissed them, Dori fled
as if pursued by ravening wolves.

Back in the coveted room, the ivy-covered
academy walls that had looked so pictur-

esque in the advertisement closed in on Dori. She slowly removed the white dress, its charm besmirched by the unpleasant Miss Brookings and her flock of simpering sheep. She hung it at the back of the wardrobe and donned the drab uniform. It changed her from a cattle rancher's sister into one of the sheep. Dori shuddered. *She, a sheep? Never — unless it were a black sheep.*

Footsteps followed by low voices sounded outside Dori's door. Ears made keen from the need to be alert while riding the range, she tiptoed to the door and opened it a crack. The hall was dimly lit, but Dori recognized the girl who had questioned her at the table, huddled in a circle with two other girls.

"Just who is this Dolores Sterling, anyway?" Harriet challenged.

"She's no lady in spite of her fancy clothes and airs," a second girl said.

"That's right," the third agreed. "Look how tan she is. Ladies are known by how white their skin is." A quickly stifled giggle sounded.

"She looks Mexican to me. Besides, Dolores is a Spanish name, isn't it?" Harriet's tone was so spiteful it set Dori afire with anger. "So what is *she* doing at Brookside?

My parents didn't send me here to hobnob with foreigners. And," she added, "whatever are the van Dykes going to say?"

Dori threw caution to the winds and flung the door wide open. "The van Dykes can go hang." Hands on her hips, a cauldron of hot words trembled just behind her tongue, threatening to burst out and scorch her adversaries. "I am not —" A daring thought halted her denial. She scornfully raised her head. There wasn't a drop of Spanish blood in her, but why not capitalize on her name and her ink-black hair?

"My name is Dolores Sterling. I am not a foreigner. However, you may call me the *Spanish señorita* — and the last thing I intend to do is to hobnob, as you so inelegantly put it, with either you or the van Dykes." Ignoring the collective gasp that followed her bold announcement, Dori turned on her heel and marched back into her room. She slammed the door with a resounding *thud,* rejoicing over the shocked faces she'd left staring at her, but also feeling guilty.

I didn't say I was Spanish, God, she said, salving her conscience. *Only that they could call me señorita. Besides, what if I were Spanish? Solita and my Mexican friends are worth far more than this bunch of East Coast nin-*

35

nies. What am I doing here, anyway?

In the days that followed, Dori asked herself the same question over and over. She hated the regimentation and ached for wide open spaces. She despised the gray dresses and white pinafores Miss Brookings's "young ladies" were forced to wear. "Life is worse than the stories Captain Perry Mace used to tell about the discipline of military life," she often told herself.

Too proud to admit defeat and go home like a frightened calf bawling for its mother, Dori decided to seek revenge. One look at Miss Used-to-Having-Her-Own-Way van Dyke, on whom Miss Brookings openly fawned, and Dori determined to oust "dear Gretchen" from first place in the academic standings. Thanks to an excellent teacher in Madera and Matt's insistence that his sister always do her best, Dori was well prepared to carry out her plan.

The first marking period established a running competition between the girls. Dori edged Gretchen into second place in every class except deportment.

"Why should I be penalized for breaking rules that make no sense?" Dori complained to Scraggs. "Why am I forbidden to climb out my window and down the ivy on starlit nights? I hate being cooped up, and I'm not hurting anyone." She scowled. "Janey overheard Gretchen — the sneak — report me. Tale bearing is far worse than what I do."

Scraggs looked sympathetic. "It is to you . . . or to me," he whispered, "but what we think doesn't count. Gossip has it that Miss Gretchen is Miss Brookings's pet student. She hasn't forgiven you for being in 'her' room, you know. I hear things." His smile made Dori wonder why she had ever considered him gloomy.

Scraggs glanced around the hall as if fearful of being overheard. "Mr. van Dyke's coffers are very well filled, you know." He patted Dori's shoulder. "Don't fret about it. I understand your . . . uh . . . pranks are winning admiration from some of the other young ladies." His posture remained as rigid as ever, but a telltale gleam in his pale eyes betrayed his approval. "Of course, Misses Brookings and van Dyke can't have that."

Dori felt a bit better until she was called on the carpet again the next day.

The Babbling Brook wore her wrinkled-prune face. "Why must you be so impertinent?" she demanded. "Miss Allison says you openly challenged her authority."

Dori's lips tightened. "Anyone who states that 'the wild West is filled with uncouth persons and is not a fit place to live' needs challenging. Besides, I only quoted Exodus 20:16: 'Thou shalt not bear false witness against thy neighbour.' I could have said that westerners are at least polite enough to keep quiet about people and places they have never seen and know absolutely nothing about."

The woman's face turned purple. "What do you mean?"

Dori clenched her hands into fists. "Yesterday Miss Allison said I was fortunate to have escaped the Indian massacres by coming here. I had to set her straight. It's been years since any California Indians went on the warpath."

The headmistress made a strangling sound and waved toward the door. "You may go, but if you feel the need to correct an instructor from now on, do it privately and respectfully."

"I *was* respectful." Resentment shot through Dori. "I thought Brookside Finishing School for Young Ladies wanted its students to know the truth, not lies. It says so right in our list of rules. 'The Bible is the great rule of duty for both teachers and scholars. Truth and virtue, Christian kindness and courtesy will be the governing principle of conduct to all the members of this school.' Am I wrong? Or don't the teachers practice what the rule preaches?"

"Go!" Miss Brookings thundered.

Dori flounced out — and received another failing mark in deportment.

FIVE

An unexpected holiday offered Dori temporary respite from her troubles. Filled with anticipation instead of dread, she bounded out of bed on the Friday set aside to honor the settling of Boston: September 17, 1880, the city's 250th birthday celebration.

Dori had written to Matt as little as possible, for fear he would know how miserable she was. How could she tell him her only real friends were the butler and a maid?

"Scraggs doesn't dare show he likes me for fear of losing his position. Janey works so hard she seldom has time for fun," Dori lamented. "Well, now at least I'll have something interesting to write about. It's too bad Matt can't be here. He'd like it, I know." A pang went through her, but she shook off regret and determined to make the most of the holiday.

Dori had never seen such a spectacle. Chaperoned by teachers and forced to remain with the other girls, she stared open-mouthed as 14,500 people marched four and a half miles, amidst a multitude of decorations. The march took three and a half hours. Several of the Brookside young ladies grew tired and went back to the school, but Dori couldn't bear to miss anything. Fortunately, one of the teachers displayed equal enthusiasm, and Miss Brookings allowed Dori to remain in her charge.

That evening sixteen floats and a thousand torchbearers paraded, illuminating the streets of the city. Dori fell asleep with a happy heart for the first time since she had arrived in Boston. The next day she wrote to Matt and Solita:

I saw Mayor Frederick O. Prince. He had requested citizens to close their stores and places of business in honor of the anniversary. At a gathering at the Old South Meeting House, he stated, "The sea has been converted into land; the hills have been leveled — the valleys filled up, the sites of the Indian wigwams are now those of the palaces of our merchant princes." I suppose the van Dykes occupy one of those palaces. It made me sad for the Indians who once

41

lived here. . . .

By the grace of God and sheer willpower, Dori stayed in school. As time passed, she noticed that her independent attitude was winning grudging respect. Her teachers seldom challenged her. Some of her more daring classmates showed signs of having backbone and standing up to queen bee Gretchen van Dyke. A few tentatively offered friendship. Dori suspected this enraged Miss Brookings, but she also knew Matt continued to send generous contributions to offset his sister's shenanigans. Why worry? Nothing she did hurt anyone or anything — except her deportment mark.

Dori got a great deal of secret amusement from observing how Gretchen ignored her. Gretchen and her hangers-on swept by the "Spanish señorita" as if Dori didn't exist. But after she bested Gretchen for still another marking period, Gretchen accosted her in the upper hall, backed up by Harriet and a few other girls.

"I've had as much as I am going to take from you, Dolores Sterling," she spat out. Her pale eyebrows arched over her washed-out blue eyes until she resembled an angry cat with its back up. "You think you're so smart. Well, you aren't. The only way you could ever get better marks than I is by cheating."

The unfair accusation left Dori speechless, but only for a moment. Rage started at her toes and engulfed her body. She clenched her fists and took a menacing step closer to her accuser. "I have never cheated in my whole life, Miss van Dyke. I don't have to cheat to be first in my studies with you as competition." She stopped for breath then added, "Stop your whining."

Gretchen fell back, face paper-white. "Miss Brookings will hear about your impertinence."

"I'm sure she will." Dori spun on one heel, pushed open the door to her room, and whirled back toward the group of cowering young ladies. "Just be sure when you run bleating to Miss Brookings that you tell her who started this. If you don't, I will." She shriveled the other girls with a lightning glance. "There must be at least *one* person here who won't lie for you." She entered her room and slammed the door behind her.

To Dori's amazement, Miss Brookings said nothing about the confrontation. Had Gretchen's followers convinced her it wouldn't be wise to report it? Perhaps. But the ill-concealed enmity in Gretchen's face showed she was lying in wait like a cougar stalking a fawn, ready to strike when the opportunity arose.

In late November, Dori made the hardest decision of her life, so startling she felt it necessary to justify it to Matt, to herself, and to God.

"If I go home for the holidays or for summer vacations, I will never come back. I won't be able to tear myself away from home," she told the Lord. "The only way to finish what I started is to stay put."

She agonized over what to say in her letter, but finally settled on writing:

Once I return home, I won't be back, so I should see everything I can while I'm here. There will be other girls staying as well. Scraggs says it isn't so bad. The teachers who remain during school breaks get up excursions for those of us who don't go home. Not just in Boston, but to other cities, as well — perhaps Philadelphia or New York. Maybe even to Washington. I know you will be disappointed. So am I, but the best thing is for me to stay.

Love to everyone,
Dori

Dori was forced to copy her letter three

times. If Matt saw a tear-splotched edition, he would order her home posthaste.

Dori remained adamant in her decision, in spite of Matt's continued protests. She dug in her heels and made it through two seemingly endless years, hating the freezing winters and longing for Madera's mild climate.

Propped up in bed one late fall day in 1882, she mused, "I can last one more school year. After spring term, I'll leave Boston to Miss Brookings and the van Dykes and their ilk." A familiar feeling of jealousy that had been nagging her for months dimmed her expectations for going home. Dori sighed. "I don't feel I've changed, but things won't be the same on the Diamond S."

She punched her pillows into a more comfortable position. "It's bad enough that for the past two years Matt's letters have been filled with praise for that . . . that Seth Anderson. Matt acts like the dumb cowhand is a long-lost brother and not simply hired help." She blew out a breath. "I suppose it's because Matt saved his life." Dori slid out of bed and crossed to the window. "Worse, now Matt's crazy about Seth's sister. According to his letters, Sarah is one in a million and 'a paragon of virtue.' "

Dori viciously dug the toe of her slipper into the carpet. "I want Matt to myself when I get home, not dancing attendance on some girl who sounds too good to be true." She raised her gaze to the ceiling. "Of course I'm sorry for what Sarah's stepfather put her through, God, but what if she's after Matt because he owns the largest spread in the valley? What if she breaks his heart the way Lydia Hensley did?"

Dori chilled. Had she made a terrible mistake by staying in Boston so long? Had Matt turned to the Andersons for the companionship he and Dori used to share?

She knelt beside the window and bowed her head. "I need to know what to do, God. Should I chuck school and go home?" The idea caught fire until she was ready to pack her clothes and take the first train west. "Lord, if I were home, I could halt any schemes Seth and Sarah Anderson may have to worm themselves into Matt's life and the Diamond S."

Six

Late fall, 1882
San Joaquin Valley

Seth Anderson stamped into the living room of the Diamond S ranch house. "Here's the mail, Boss. Curly just got back from Madera." He tossed the bundle to Matt, who was sprawled in a comfortable chair, staring at Seth's sister, Sarah. Light from the blazing logs in the fireplace turned her hair to glistening gold and brought the colors of the gorgeous Mexican wall tapestries alive.

Seth hunkered down in front of the huge rock fireplace and grinned. *Looks like one of these days I'm gonna have me a brother-in-law.* He glanced at their beloved housekeeper, who gave him a knowing smile. *I bet Solita thinks the same thing.*

"Thanks, Seth." Matt riffled through the mail and looked disappointed. "Nothing from Dori." He frowned. "Another letter from the Brookside headmistress, though.

Wonder what my dear sister has been up to this time? And how much it's going to cost me to keep her in school."

Seth set his lips in a straight line and fought the irritation any mention of Dolores Sterling always generated. The girl had left for some high-falutin' school back east two years earlier — shortly before Matt saved Seth's life and brought him to the ranch. In Seth's opinion, Matt's sister was a spoiled brat and one of the few things that kept life on the Diamond S from being near perfect.

He sent a fleeting look at the large picture that adorned the mantel of the hacienda-style ranch house. How could such an innocent-looking girl be so devilish and cause a grand fellow like Matt endless trouble?

Seth's heart swelled with indignation. Dori seldom wrote and refused to come home from her precious school for vacations and holidays. Yet the picture of the feminine replica of dark-haired Matt held a certain fascination. "Sure not like what happened with Matt and Sarah," Seth muttered under cover of poking the fireplace logs until they crackled and blazed.

His annoyance vanished. He had "innocently" supplied Matt and Sarah photographs of each other in a clumsy attempt at matchmaking. The photographs had done their work well. Attraction sprang up between his sister and his boss before they ever met. Seth grinned. The chance of him doing likewise and falling in love with Dori's picture was the most ridiculous thing he could imagine.

Matt slapped his leg and howled with mirth.

It stopped Seth's woolgathering. "What's so funny?"

"Dori." Matt whooped again. "She's done it this time. I know I should be furious, but it's just too —" He broke into gales of laughter. "Listen to this." He wiped away tears and began to read. " 'Dear Mr. Sterling, it gives me no pleasure to be the bearer of bad news yet again, but something must be done about your sister. I realize how important it is to you for Dolores to remain at Brookside, and I have bent over backward to accommodate you.' " Matt stopped reading and snorted. "Hogwash. Any bending over backward is because of my money."

Seth silently agreed but kept his own counsel. He didn't dare look at Sarah for fear she'd discern what he was thinking. She'd warned Seth never to let Matt know how he

49

felt about Dolores. "In many ways," she reminded him on many occasions, "Matt looks at you as a replacement for his dead brother, Robbie. He would be heartbroken to know your feelings about his sister are less than charitable."

Seth ducked his head and stared at the floor, torn between loyalty to his boss and the unholy desire to give Dori Sterling the tongue-lashing he felt she richly deserved.

"Go on, Señor Mateo," Solita urged, hands clasped tightly.

" 'Mr. Sterling, I regret to inform you that Dolores's recent behavior is unacceptable and brings dishonor to the name of my fine establishment. It pains me to relate such an unseemly matter, but I feel I must. One of my young ladies, Gretchen van Dyke, has shown true Christian charity regarding the change of rooms. Your sister, however, continues to spitefully plague and belittle dear Gretchen and undermine her leadership among the other girls.' "

Seth chuckled. The headmistress sounded like someone out of a dime novel, with her fine airs and pompous "regrets" about criticizing Dori. It looked to Seth like Dori and Gretchen were cut from the same cloth and deserved each other. But he kept his opinion to himself.

Matt raised a skeptical eyebrow. "I'll eat my Stetson if Gretchen van Dyke ever showed Christian charity, especially to Dori." He continued reading. " 'I have been patient, but your sister's latest indignity toward Gretchen cannot be brushed aside. Dear Gretchen found a little black cat mewing outside in the rain. Too kind to leave it there, she begged to be allowed to keep it, even though pets are normally forbidden. I didn't have the heart to say no, so I reluctantly agreed. I also explained to the other girls that kindness to animals is akin to biblical teachings about treating with compassion those less fortunate.

" 'Dolores had the audacity to remind me of my reprimand when she fed a stray dog, which, of course, is not the same thing at all.' "

Seth felt an unexpected twinge of pity for Dori. It didn't lessen his annoyance with her for treating Matt shabbily, but anyone who fed a stray dog couldn't be all bad. "What a hypocrite Miss Brookings is," he burst out. "No wonder Dori plays tricks."

"She certainly did this time. It looks like Dori sneaked into 'dear Gretchen's' room, swiped the cat, and" — Matt chortled —

51

"wait till you hear what happened next: 'Several of the girls and teachers were gathered in the drawing room for a musicale. Gretchen was at the piano. The door opened. A ghastly-looking beast darted in, closely followed by Dolores.

" 'Some of the girls screamed. Then your sister said, "What is that?" She pointed to the creature, and a look of horror crossed her face. She frightened everyone with her next words. "Oh, Miss Brookings, I do hope it isn't a hydrophobic skunk. We have them out west. Sometimes skunks go mad. If they bite people, the people also go mad . . . and die." ' "

This was too much for Seth. He rolled on the floor and cackled. Blessed with a vivid imagination, he could picture the scene: Miss Brookings, an assembly of people, and an unrepentant Dori. The others joined in, but at last Matt controlled himself and went on. " 'Dear Gretchen swooned, striking her head on the piano. The other girls leaped onto the furniture.

" 'Fortunately, Scraggs heard the commotion and came to the rescue. He bravely picked up the beast and discovered it was dear Gretchen's cat. Someone had painted a white stripe down its back. All evidence pointed to Dolores as the instigator of this cruel deception.

" 'She confessed immediately and showed not the slightest remorse for her actions. Needless to say, Dolores is confined to her room except for meals and classes." ' "

Matt tossed the letter into the fire. "What does Miss Brookings expect me to do about this?" He sighed. "I suppose another bank draft will help the woman simmer down. It always does." He looked shamefaced. "I can't wait to tell the hands — and Brett, too. My foreman is as guilty of spoiling Dori as I am, and this is too good to keep to ourselves. They'll all get a chuckle over it."

Solita leaned forward, face earnest. "It is like Señorita Dolores to play tricks, especially on those who are unkind to her."

"If you remember, she wanted to go," Matt said. "Nothing is keeping her there."

Solita shook her head. "Her pride, Señor Mateo."

"Maybe I should relieve Miss Brookings of her burden and bring Dori home."

"No!"

Seth couldn't believe he'd blurted it out. What business was it of his what the boss did with his rebellious sister?

Before he could answer, Sarah spoke for

the first time. "I agree with Seth. Evidently Dori has determined to finish her course. She must be allowed to do so."

Solita nodded. "*Sí.* This year will pass, and Dolores will come home to our casa." Her deep brown eyes glistened. "We shall laugh and sing and give thanks to *Dios.*"

The depths of love reflected in Solita's face stirred Seth. Why couldn't Dori see what she was doing to those who loved her? She was eighteen now, the same age Sarah had been when she fled St. Louis to avoid being sold in marriage to a riverboat gambler. Far too old to be playing childish tricks.

The girls were so different. Both had spunk, but Sarah's faith in God kept her in check. Everything Seth knew about Dori indicated she was a raging, out-of-control river. According to the hands, she ruled the ranch with a rod of charm.

She won't rule me. I'll keep as far away from her as possible, Seth decided. He sobered. Once the bothersome girl came home, nothing on the Diamond S would ever be the same.

Seven

Three thousand miles from Madera, trouble blew in from across the Atlantic. It started when the Babbling Brook, more atwitter than usual, announced, "I have the most wonderful news." For once color tinted her pale face, and a sparkle glimmered in her eyes. "Stancel Worthington III is coming to Brookside from London. Dear Stancel is my very own nephew, but he has always been more like my son. He will teach dancing."

A pleased smile crept over her face at the murmur of interest among the girls. It broadened when Gretchen van Dyke trilled, "Oh, Miss Brookings, how exciting!"

Dori's lip curled. How could anyone get excited over one of the Babbling Brook's relatives, especially one named Stancel Worthington III? *Wonder if anyone ever calls him Mr. Third,* she thought. *He is probably as stuffy as his name.*

Stuffy didn't begin to describe the new dancing master. The day he arrived, Dori had just checked the upper hall to make sure she was alone, then taken a glorious slide down the banister rail. She crashed into Stancel at full speed. If the huge front doors had been open, she would have knocked him out of them.

He lurched back, yet all he said when she landed in a heap on the marble floor was, "Upon my word, what have we here?"

Dori gawked at the man struggling to regain his footing. For once, she didn't speak. She dared not. One hand flew to her open mouth to keep from laughing. She knew she looked ridiculous sprawled on the floor, but not nearly as absurd as Miss Brookings's newly arrived nephew.

Tall and meticulously dressed in the latest men's fashion, "dear Stancel" could have hung a lantern on his aristocratic, hooked nose. Neatly combed black hair — each strand in place — peeked out from beneath a bowler hat. He seemed at a loss but quickly regained his composure and offered Dori a flabby, pasty hand. "I say, miss, that was quite a —"

"Sorry," Dori interrupted, scrambling to her feet. She ignored his outstretched hand and fled back up the stairs two at a time.

Once in her room, she threw herself on the bed and released her bottled-up laughter. "Judged against the men and boys back home, he makes a mighty poor showing." She wiped away tears of amusement. Then a new thought suffocated her laughter. "This . . . this . . . insipid Englishman is my dancing teacher?" Dori groaned. The thought of Mr. Worthington's pale hand taking hers in a dance was repugnant.

Dori had dreaded the class, but Stancel's presence made it pure torment. Give her a good, old-fashioned barn dance any day, not the mincing steps and low curtseys Mr. Worthington insisted the girls learn. She avoided him as much as possible and secretly rejoiced when he paid Gretchen marked attentions, to the obvious delight of Miss Brookings.

Alas for Dori! Her indifference evidently pricked Stancel's pride. He began ignoring Gretchen and choosing Dori for a partner. Stumbling and stepping on his feet did no good. The more she attempted to escape the dancing master's unwelcome attentions, the more persistent he grew. In addition, what little civility existed between Dori and "dear Gretchen" suffered a total collapse.

Things came to a head in early December, a few days after Matt summoned his sister home for his and Sarah's wedding. He wrote:

When that scoundrel Red Fallon conspired with Sarah's stepfather and kidnapped her, I knew she might be lost to me forever. I vowed then and there that if God would help me find and save her, I'd marry Sarah as soon as she'd set a date.

It wasn't a surprise, but Dori still felt she'd been hit by a train. She'd long since given up the idea of rushing home to save Matt from the Andersons. But in spite of sympathy for Sarah, the thought that never again would Matt be all hers — as he had been since their father, mother, and Robbie died — hurt intolerably.

She looked out the window into a cheerless day, her spirits at their lowest ebb. "Maybe it won't be so hard coming back to school in January after all," she whispered. "Sarah might not want me at the ranch, even though her own precious brother, Seth, is more than welcome."

Torn by emotion, she was in no mood for a confrontation with Gretchen van Dyke. When the fiery-eyed girl burst into Dori's room and slammed the door behind her,

58

Dori demanded, "Don't you have manners enough to knock?"

Gretchen's face mottled. "I know what you are up to."

Dori had never seen Gretchen so distraught. "Anything I may be up to doesn't concern you."

"Indeed it does." Gretchen raved. "Stancel Worthington is mine, do you hear?"

"Lower your voice or half of Boston will hear you," Dori retorted. "I have no interest whatsoever in your property, if that's what he is."

"Rubbish! Miss Brookings told me Stancel is determined to turn the Spanish señorita into a lady, and marry her. Miss Brookings is outraged — and so am I," she sputtered.

Dori sprang to her feet. She clenched her hands until the nails bit into her palms. "Not half as outraged as I am. You think I'd marry that English codfish? Never!"

Before Gretchen could answer, someone knocked at the door. "Miss Dolores?"

"Come in, Janey."

The maid opened the door and stepped inside. Every freckle stood out on her frightened face. "Miss Brookings says you are to come to her office immediately."

"Thank you, Janey." Dori waited until the

girl scuttled away, then rounded on Gretchen. "Now get out of my room or you'll be sorry."

Gretchen smirked. "You're the one who is going to be sorry. Miss Brookings will surely put you in your place once and for all." She flounced out.

Now what? Dori wondered. She had kept out of Miss Brookings's way since the cat incident, and only a short time remained until she would go home for the wedding. How ironic for fate to ambush her just after she had schooled herself to come back for the spring term.

Miss Brookings sat behind her desk; her nephew lounged in a chair beside her. One look told Dori that the headmistress was loaded for bear and ready to fire.

"Of all the shameless hussies, you are the worst, Dolores Sterling. Coquetting with dear Stancel, leading him on, and brazenly attempting to weasel your way into society by underhanded means. Let me tell you this, young woman. Stancel will marry you only over my dead body."

"I say. It's not very cricket for you to disapprove before I have declared my intentions," Stancel protested.

Dori's heart slammed against her chest. She glared at her accuser and discharged both barrels of her fury. "What makes you think I would even consider being courted by a skim-milk specimen like Stancel?" she blazed. "God willing, if or when I marry, it will be to someone who is pure cream, not a whey-faced sissy like your nephew."

"Get out," the headmistress demanded. "Pack your clothes. You will leave immediately. Go — and never darken the door of Brookside Finishing School for Young Ladies again."

"You couldn't pay me to stay after this," Dori said scornfully. "I can't wait to tell my brother how I have been insulted. As for you" — she rounded on Stancel, who was gaping like a fish out of water — "if you were in Madera, the Diamond S hands would make quick work of you." Dori sailed out the open door, leaving stone-cold silence behind her. But before she turned a corner, she heard Stancel say, "Jove, but she's magnificent. It makes a man want to —"

Dori neither heard nor cared what Stancel Worthington III wanted to do. All she wanted to do was to shake the dust of Brookside Finishing School for Young Ladies from her shoes and take the first train west.

Dori's outrage and humiliation sustained

61

her through her final hours in Boston. If it hadn't been for Janey, Dori's clothing would have reached Madera in sad condition.

"Let me help you," the little maid pleaded when Dori began tossing dresses helter-skelter into her trunks. Her eyes twinkled as she pointed to a stack of uniforms. "You'll not be wanting these, I suspect."

Dori glared at the garments that represented the mountain of indignities she had suffered for two years. "Keep the pinafores if you like, but tear up those ugly grey dresses and use them to scrub the floors." Dori thought for a moment. She would soon be gone, but why not fire a parting shot? One that would echo through the halls and ensure she would not soon be forgotten. Her heart raced with anticipation. "I have a better idea," she gleefully told Janey.

The maid cocked her head. "What are you up to, miss?"

"Deliver the dresses to Gretchen van Dyke when I'm gone." Dori seized writing materials, quickly scribbled a note, and read it aloud. "What do you think of this? 'Gretchen, the Bible says to do good to them that hate you. And to pray for them which despitefully use you and persecute you. You can have *my room* and my castoff uniforms. You can also have Stancel, if you aren't too proud to take a man I don't want any more than I want these secondhand uniforms. The Spanish *señorita.*"

Janey went into a fit of giggles. "Miss Gretchen will have an attack of the vapors," she predicted. "But oh, what a perfect way for you to have the last word."

Dori exploded with delight and felt suddenly lighthearted. Miss Brookings's untrue accusations still rankled, but knowing she had again bested "dear Gretchen" had released some of Dori's anger and humiliation.

The girls barely finished packing before a tap came at the door. "The carriage is here to take you to the station, Miss Dolores," Scraggs called. "And the men to carry your trunks down."

A rush of thankfulness for the butler's surreptitious friendship filled Dori. She flung the door open and threw her arms around his stiff, unbending frame. "I'm going to miss you," she told him. "You and Janey."

He coughed and smiled down at her, correct as ever but with warmth in his eyes. "And I, you, Miss Dori. I fear there will be no more incidents to liven up this rather staid place." His droll observation sent the two girls into peals of laughter, but he quickly shushed them. Then he led the way downstairs and into a day as gray and gloomy as the one on which Dori had arrived.

Her final glimpse of the prison of her own making was of Scraggs and Janey waving to her from outside the forbidding doors.

EIGHT

Clackety-clack. Clackety-clack. Each turn of the westbound train's wheels took Dori farther away from the scene of her disgrace and closer to the Diamond S. Exhilaration over getting in the final lick at Gretchen van Dyke kept her spirits high. When the train reached the outskirts of Boston, Dori studied the last of the tall buildings that had threatened to squeeze the life out of her.

"Good riddance to bad rubbish," she exulted. Yet niggling unease set in. Every incident had consequences. Was being expelled when she was innocent retribution for all the times she'd been guilty? Because of Matt's forbearance, she'd never paid a high price for her previous escapades.

Dori scooted down in her seat. "What is Matt going to say about this fiasco?" she whispered. "He will be furious with Stancel, but he's bound to be disappointed in me. He spent all that money, and now I won't even graduate." Shame scorched her, and her thoughts rushed on. *If I hadn't broken rules and made Miss Brookings hate me, she wouldn't have accused me of trying to ensnare her pompous nephew.*

Righteous indignation temporarily killed Dori's self-chastisement. No red-blooded American girl would want milk-and-water Stancel Worthington III, at least none she knew. Too bad he didn't come out west and meet some real men. Curly, Bud, Slim — even Red Fallon, rotten as he was — made "dear Stancel" look sick. And if what Matt said about Seth Anderson were true, the young cowboy would cast a mighty tall shadow over the insufferable Englishman. Anger gave way to mirth. Dori could just imagine Stancel's reaction to being compared with a bunch of cowboys, let alone kidnapper and scourge of the range Red Fallon.

An outrageous plan gripped her unrepentant mind. "Why don't I get even with Miss Brookings by inviting her precious nephew to visit the ranch? Boy, would he get his comeuppance." She snickered and felt excitement mount. "The Diamond S outfit would laugh his high-and-mightiness off the range." Dori sighed and reluctantly dismissed the idea. Stancel's parting words —

"I say, but she's magnificent. It makes a man want to . . ." — had sent warning chills up and down her spine. The farther she stayed away from Stancel Worthington III, the better.

As the train chugged its way west, depression set in. The thought of having to tell Matt hung over Dori and troubled her conscience. "Just like the sword of Damocles," she muttered.

"Pardon me, miss, do you need something?"

She turned from the window and gazed into the face peering down at her. "No. I was just mumbling to myself."

"You said something about a sword?" the conductor asked.

She nodded. "Yes, the sword of Damocles."

An interested gleam crept into his gray eyes. "Begging your pardon, but what might that be?"

"A story from my history book. Damocles was a member of the court of Dionysius II, who ruled in Sicily before the birth of Christ. The Roman orator Cicero said Damocles was a flatterer, forever talking about Dionysius's happiness and good fortune. To teach him a lesson, Dionysius gave a great feast. He dangled a sword over

Damocles' head. It was suspended by a single hair."

The conductor's eyebrows shot up. "Did it ever fall?"

"History or legend doesn't say." Dori burned with anger. "But it just fell on me."

The conductor patted her gloved hand. "It can't be that bad."

Dori gulped. "It's worse. I just got fired, I mean expelled, from Brookside Finishing School for Young Ladies. It wasn't even my fault."

A wise expression creased the conductor's face. "Oh, that place. Rumor has it the headmistress is a tartar. I reckon you aren't the first and won't be the last to cross swords with her." He smiled. "Cheer up, miss, and look out there." He pointed to the window. "My old mother always said things didn't seem so bad when the sun was shining. The rain's letting up now, so 'twon't surprise me if we see a rainbow." He touched his cap and moved down the aisle.

Dori took heart from the conductor's comments . . . and from the glorious rainbow that split the sky. "Thank You, God," she whispered. She watched until creeping dusk swallowed the last shimmering remnants of the rainbow before stirring herself

68

to go to the dining car for a long-delayed supper.

Whenever the conductor could spare a moment from his duties, he hovered over Dori like a mama cat over her kittens. He expressed indignation when she told him of Stancel's intentions and Miss Brookings's allegations. He also chortled about Dori's final message to "dear Gretchen." Although he looked nothing like Scraggs, Dori appreciated the same kindly concern the butler had shown her.

Before they reached Chicago, Dori confessed her previous experience in the train station. Fear surged up inside her and dried her mouth. "I'm just afraid it might happen again," she confided to the conductor. "It was all so confusing with people pushing and shoving me. This time I don't have Matt to rescue me."

"Don't you be fretting, miss. I'll see to it that you don't get left behind," her new friend promised. He kept his word, both in Chicago and at the other stops along the way. But after they reached Denver and were well into the snow-clogged mountains, an anxious look replaced his usual caring expression. "When did you say your brother's wedding was to take place?"

Dori felt wings of apprehension brush

against her nerves. "On Christmas Day. Why?"

He shook his head. "It doesn't look good. We just got word that avalanches ahead are causing delays." Worry lines creased his forehead. "We may have to turn back."

"We can't go back," Dori protested, appalled by the idea. "If I'm not there for Matt's wedding, he will never forgive me." *Even though you know in your heart it's the last place you want to be,* a little voice mocked.

"Surely they will postpone it. They know you're coming, don't they?"

Dori clasped her gloved hands. "Yes, but not which train I'm on. I was in such a hurry when I left Boston, I forgot to send a telegram."

"That's actually good," the conductor comforted. "If they don't know you're on this particular train, they won't be concerned about you." He scratched his head. "The only thing is, wouldn't the headmistress inform them?"

Hope died. "Probably. Although" — Dori brightened — "under the uh . . . unusual circumstances, the Babbling Brook may have decided to keep mum. She couldn't very well tell my brother I was sent home for refusing 'dear Stancel's' unwelcome ad-

70

vances."

The conductor chuckled. But he wasn't chuckling a few miles up the track. The screaming of brakes followed by a rumble and a roar brought Dori out of a sound sleep. Dazed and only half awake, she landed in the aisle amidst screams from other similarly afflicted passengers. She scrambled up, rubbed an aching elbow, and grabbed the arm of the porter, who was helping people to their feet. "What's happening?"

"Avalanche." His mouth set in a grim line. "Thank God we were traveling up instead of down. If we'd hit that pile of snow at full speed, we'd all be goners." He freed himself from Dori's frantic clutch and hurried on to assist others.

Dori's heart sank. How long would it take to get tracks cleared so they could go on? She pressed her nose to the window but saw nothing except swirling white. It made her feel even colder than during the last two winters in Boston. The door of the car burst open. A blast of freezing air rushed in. Dori shivered and huddled deeper into the blue velvet cloak she had purchased shortly after reaching Boston and discovering how miserable their winters could be. Yet in spite of its warm lining and the glowing fire in the box at the end of the car, she still felt chilly.

It seemed like hours before the conductor appeared. When he did, Dori could see in his concerned face the news was not good.

"A huge mass of snow came down on the tracks," he told the passengers.

A murmur arose, but he raised his hand. "Help is on the way, but we don't know how long it will take for them to get here and dig us out."

"Then take us back to Denver," a high-pitched, hysterical voice ordered. Others joined in, muttering complaints against the railroad, the weather, and the conductor.

Dori felt like jumping up and ordering them to be quiet, but decided prudence was more desirable than defending her new friend.

He blew out a great breath. "I'm sorry to say it won't be possible to go back. There's also been an avalanche between here and Denver."

"You mean we're trapped! We're all going to die! Why did I ever leave home?" the speaker shouted above the clamor that arose. Dori remained silent while the conductor attempted to calm the passengers' fears, but her heart echoed the frantic cry: *Why did I ever leave home?*

"Well, Lord," she prayed under cover of

the furor. "There's no use crying over spilt milk, even though the cowcatcher is evidently stuck against a mountain of snow." She shivered again and sent the beleaguered conductor what she hoped was a comforting smile. How anyone could blame him for an act of God was beyond her.

"If you'll give me a shovel, I'll help dig," she told him. He just laughed and shook his head before going on to the next car.

The train remained snowbound all night. Unable to fall asleep again, Dori had ample time to consider her precarious position. She might miss the wedding, but unless help came, she and others could lose their lives. The conductor had reported that a work train was being sent to them from the next station, but how long would it take to get there? What if other avalanches came? They could be buried alive.

Dori's fear of being confined in small spaces rose to haunt her. She paced the aisle when it was clear, silently asking God to deliver them. She also reached a decision. *Even if I reach Madera in time for the wedding, I won't let anyone at the Diamond S know I've been expelled. There will be time enough when Matt and Sarah return from their San Francisco honeymoon for them to learn I won't be going back.*

Dori groaned. Although she vowed not to spoil Matt's special day, the secret hanging over her was almost more than she could bear. She refused to consider what she'd do if Sarah disliked her and didn't want her on the ranch. Right now, surviving the avalanche was the most important thing in Dori's world.

Late the next morning, the beaming conductor appeared, "Good news, folks. The work train is here, and it looks like we will be on our way in a few hours." Loud cheers resounded through the train.

Most of the passengers let out whoops of joy. But a few well-dressed men continued to complain. They threatened to write to the railroad company, their congressmen, and even President Chester A. Arthur about the "inexcusable inconvenience and suffering" caused by the delay.

Dori had had enough. She leaped to her feet and faced the grumblers, feeling hot blood rush to her face. Scorn dripped from her unruly tongue. "I didn't hear any of you offering to lend a hand."

"Did you?" a portly man who looked like he'd never done a day's hard work barked.

"She sure did." A wide grin spread over the conductor's seamed face. "As soon as this spunky young lady knew about our

74

predicament, she volunteered to help dig us out if I'd give her a shovel."

Laughter echoed throughout the car. The man who had challenged Dori subsided, and peace was restored.

Once the train was free to go on its way, there were no more delays. After what felt like an eternity, the *clackety-clack* of the great wheels slowed and stopped at the Madera station.

The prodigal sister had come home.

NINE

"Ride 'em, cowboy." Curly's stentorian yell, accompanied by raucous laughter from Bud and Slim, who were perched next to him on the top rail of the Diamond S corral, made Seth Anderson grin. He leaned forward in the saddle, tightened his legs against the pinto mare's sides, and waited for the next buck. The mare obliged, but after a few half-hearted pitches she stopped short, turned her head, and surveyed her rider as if to say she'd had enough.

"Easiest horse I ever broke," Seth mumbled. "Open the gate," he called to the heckling trio. "I'll give her a good run and see what kind of ginger she has."

Curly whooped and sprang to obey. Seth and the mare raced out of the corral and down the road toward Madera as if pursued by a grizzly bear. Wind whistled in his ears and he bent over the horse's neck. "Go, Splotches. I'll eat my Stetson if Dori Sterling isn't crazy about you. Matt couldn't have found a better Christmas present for her."

He laughed. "You're a far cry from the nags Dori's probably been forced to straddle in Boston. Riding sidesaddle, bound up tight in a fancy riding habit, and plodding along at some fool ladylike trot? She may as well have been riding a rocking chair." The freedom of the range surged through Seth and aroused his pity for Dori. It must have been frustrating for a girl used to the wide-open spaces to be so constrained. "Say, Splotches, if she isn't thrilled with you, I'll keep you myself. You're the prettiest little pinto in the country, and you move right along."

The mare's ears pricked up. She stretched into a ground-covering gallop. Seth let her run, feeling wild and free, the way he had ever since coming to the ranch. At last he reined Splotches in beneath a huge oak tree. "Time to take a breather." He slid from the saddle and patted the mare's neck. She rewarded him by rubbing her nose against Seth's shoulder. Would Dori appreciate the pinto? He hoped so for Matt's sake.

He stroked Splotches' mane. "No matter. She'll be heading back to Boston after the wedding, and I'll ride you." He chuckled. "Just so Copper doesn't get jealous." Seth's happiness faded. His faithful sorrel gelding, companion and friend for many years, had stepped in a gopher hole a few weeks earlier and pulled a ligament.

"My fault," Seth grumbled. "I should have been paying attention instead of thinking about Dori coming home." The swelling on Copper's leg had been reduced with hot packs, and Matt said the horse would be fine, but Seth's guilt remained. Now he raised his head, removed his wide hat, and gazed into the blue December sky. He watched a hawk circle in the clear air before confessing, "Lord, I have an even bigger problem. I've been judging Matt's sister by the trouble she's caused him." Seth heaved a great sigh. "Even if Dori turns out to be as wayward and heedless as Matt says she is, I need to respect her because she's Your child." Seth scratched his head. "I reckon the best way to do that is to just keep out of her way." He paused and allowed the silence to fill him. "Thanks for listening, God."

Seth got to his feet and stretched. Talking with his Trailmate always made him feel better. Besides, it should be easy enough to avoid Dori for the short time she would be home without his avoidance becoming obvious.

What about when she comes home perma-

78

nently? a little voice taunted. Seth shrugged. Summer was a long way off. Anything could happen before then. He swung into the saddle and turned Splotches toward home, but the sound of hoofbeats stopped him. Seth looked back and stared at the rider. When freckle-faced Johnny Foster raced a horse like that it usually meant bad news.

"Trouble, Johnny?" Seth called.

"Yeah." The boy pulled his horse to a stop. "Evan Moore said to get this telegram to Matt right away. Evan told me what it says. Miss Dori is on her way home, but that ain't all." He gasped for breath. "Evan got word the train is stuck in the mountains somewhere this side of Denver. Avalanches are blocking the tracks. The message said the railroad don't know how long it will be till they can get a work train and crew there and dig the passenger train out."

Seth's heart turned to ice. "Give me the telegram. My horse is fresher than yours."

"Okay, Seth." Johnny handed it over. "I sure hope those folks, 'specially Miss Dori, get rescued real quick. It'd be awful if she has to miss Matt and Sarah's wedding." He turned his horse and headed back to Madera.

Missing the wedding is nothing compared with what could happen, Seth thought grimly.

Being trapped in a snowbound train for who knows how long could claim lives. He flinched. He'd seen snow storms cripple St. Louis. What would it be like in the Colorado mountains?

Seth goaded Splotches into a run and spoke from a heart filled with fear. "God, there's nothing any of us here can do for those stranded passengers and the crew. Please deliver them." A scripture learned in childhood crept into Seth's mind. Moses, reminding his people of God's goodness to Jacob, said: *"He found him in a desert land, and in the waste howling wilderness . . . he kept him as the apple of his eye."*

"Lord, be with everyone on that train and those sent to rescue them," Seth prayed. "Keep them as You kept Jacob. They are also in a howling wilderness and desperately need You." He paused and whispered, "In Jesus' name, amen."

The time between leaving Johnny and reaching the Diamond S felt like an eternity. When Seth and Splotches thundered up to the corral, Seth leaped to the ground, threw the mare's reins to one of the vaqueros and ordered, "Take care of her, will you?" Then he sprinted toward the ranch house. He didn't stop to knock, but burst into the hall and raced to the sitting room where Matt,

Sarah, and Solita were gathered. "Telegram. Evan sent Johnny with it."

Apprehension sprang up in Matt's eyes, and he bounded to his feet. "Now what?" He snatched the telegram, ripped it open, and read aloud,

DOLORES ON WAY HOME *Stop* LETTER FOLLOWS *Stop* GENEVIEVE BROOK-INGS.

Matt's shoulders sagged in obvious relief. "So what? Dori evidently decided to surprise us by coming earlier than planned. It's just like her."

Hatred for what he must do filled Seth. "There's bad news, Matt. The train Dori is on is snowbound west of Denver. It can't move until help gets there to dig it out."

Matt stared at him. "Dear God, no!"

Sarah echoed his prayer, but Solita put both hands over her head and wailed, "Dios be merciful to our señorita and the others."

Matt staggered to a chair and dropped into it. His shoulders shook as if he had palsy. "I don't know how Dori will stand it. Confinement in small spaces terrifies her. It always has." He groaned. "How can she stand being shut up inside a cramped railroad car with no way to escape?"

81

Sympathy for both Matt and his sister emboldened Seth. "God will be with her." His voice rang loud in the great room. "He has promised never to leave or forsake us."

"Yes," Sarah agreed. "He is our rock and our strong salvation." She knelt beside Matt and held her hands out to Seth and Solita. "We need to pray."

If Seth lived to be a hundred, he would never forget what followed. One by one, they stormed heaven on behalf of Dori and the others held in a prison of snow hundreds of miles away. The fear Seth had seen in the others' faces and felt in the air itself gradually lessened. Peace and the assurance all would be well tiptoed into Seth's heart. He raised his head. "I can't help but believe they'll be all right."

Solita and Sarah smiled. Matt gripped Seth's hand until it hurt and brokenly said, "I hope so. Now all we can do is to wait — and continue to pray."

Hours passed. Night fell. The four huddled close to the fireplace and each other. No one suggested going to bed. Seth had passed the word about Dori's predicament on to Brett Owen, and the foreman had promised to tell the hands. No good-natured banter or voices raised in cowboy songs sounded from the bunkhouse. Seth shuddered. The usually rollicking Diamond S felt like it was already in mourning. Still, he clung to the comfort that had come to him during the prayers — and continued to pray.

The dark hours passed. Dawn came. As soon as it was light enough to ride, Matt and Seth headed for Madera. They hung around Moore's General Store and Post Office until they received word that the work train had reached the passenger train and the railroad expected to have the tracks cleared in a few hours.

The bald storekeeper-postmaster's eyes twinkled. A wide grin spread across his round face. "Looks like that sister of yours will be here for the wedding, after all."

"Thank God!" Matt exclaimed, but Seth saw in Matt's eyes that the heartfelt cry of gratitude was for a lot more than Dori not missing the wedding.

The time between receiving the gladsome news and the train's arrival gave Seth the opportunity to reflect. Like it or not, his life was bound up with Dori's. Any dislike on his part was a breach of loyalty to Matt. Despite all that had happened, Seth still had misgivings about Dori and didn't want to be present when she came. But when Matt made it clear that his heart was set on Seth going to the station with him, Seth agreed.

The train pulled in. Passengers streamed off. Where was Dori? Seth's mind spun. Had Miss Brookings's telegram been wrong? Had Dori missed the train she was supposedly on? Had all of his, Matt's, Sarah's, and Solita's distress been for nothing? Seth caught sight of Matt's set jaw and clenched his hands. If that dratted girl had once again caused her brother to suffer, Seth would —

"Dori!" Matt deserted Seth and hurtled toward the train, leaving Seth to gape at the young woman daintily holding her long skirts up enough to step down from the train. The black-and-white picture on the mantel at the Diamond S had often caused Seth to wonder how such an innocent-looking girl could be so troublesome. Now that picture came alive in glorious color — and Seth wondered again. Curly dark hair peeped from beneath a stylish bonnet and framed a lovely face. Dori's sapphire velvet cloak was no bluer than her tear-filled eyes. She was one of the prettiest fillies Seth had ever seen. As pretty as his sister, Sarah, with her red-gold hair, or dark-haired, dark-eyed Abby Sheridan, who worked at the Yosemite Hotel.

Seth shook his head to clear his thoughts. Could this glorious creature whose head reached her tall brother's shoulder be the bothersome girl who had caused Matt so much worry? The girl Seth considered childish and inconsiderate? Seth's ability to size up those he met with a single lightning glance now served him well. With all her shortcomings, Dori was devoted to Matt. It showed in her eyes, in the way she flung herself into his arms, and her joyous cry, "Oh, Matt, I've missed you so much!"

Yet in spite of her obviously sincere greeting, Seth's keen gaze caught a shadow in Dori's eyes that betrayed her. All was not well. Something was disturbing the long-awaited visitor. Was Matt in for even more trouble?

TEN

Dori slid from Matt's bear hug and caught at her bonnet. The strings had come untied, and the hat threatened to slip off her head. "Don't squeeze me to death!" She threw her arms around Matt again. The bonnet slipped farther down her back. Dori didn't care. She'd missed Matt terribly. Seeing him after all this time intensified her love. He was so big and brown and strong that Dori never wanted to let him go.

Two years' worth of tears that she'd only permitted to escape in the worst circumstances threatened to gush. She shook her head to keep them from falling. The movement dislodged her bonnet; it fell to the muddy street.

Before Dori could free herself and retrieve it, a deep, rich voice spoke from behind her. "I believe this is yours."

"Dori, this is Seth Anderson," Matt said. "Seth, my sister, Dolores." The pride in his voice was so undeserved it made Dori squirm. She loosened herself from Matt's arms and turned toward the tall cowboy holding her hat in one hand and trying to remove a thick coating of dust with the other.

Dori gulped. *This* was Seth Anderson? The tenderfoot she'd convinced herself might be harboring a devious plan to hoodwink her brother? If those lake blue eyes were to be believed, he was not the villain she'd pictured.

Seth bowed, doffed his Stetson, and held out her bonnet. "Sorry I couldn't do a better job, Miss Sterling." A ray of sunshine rested on his bare head and changed his hair to molten gold, shot through with gleams of red.

The memory of Stancel gaping like a fish intruded on Dori's mind and left her speechless. Horrors! That must be how she looked now. *Don't stand here like a ninny,* she ordered herself. *It must be the sun that makes him look like the statue of a Greek god in my history book.*

Dori knew better. The light in Seth's face silently shouted it came from within. Unless looks were mighty deceiving, he was everything Matt had said and more.

An unfamiliar feeling stirred within Dori,

as if her spirit rushed out to Seth's. The thought left her shaken. She tried to toss off a bright greeting but no words came.

"Cat got your tongue?" Matt teased. "Or is Sleeping Beauty waiting for a prince to come and awaken her with a kiss?" He chuckled. "What do you think, Seth?"

If the gibe bothered Seth, he didn't show it by the flicker of an eyelash. "I think Sarah will never forgive us if we don't get Miss Sterling home. She can't wait to meet her almost-new sister." Before Matt could reply, the cowboy strode toward the pile of luggage clearly marked with Dori's name. He stopped short and shoved his Stetson back on his head. "Looks like Evan will have to send most of this stuff out in a wagon. It won't fit in the carriage."

As soon as Seth was out of earshot, Dori rounded on Matt. "How could you embarrass me like that?"

Matt donned a look of innocent surprise — the same look he always wore after besting her. He raised his palms. "What did I say?" He looked at Seth, then back at Dori. "Hey, what did you do, bring everything you owned?"

Dismay replaced Dori's exasperation. Would she have to confess then and there that she'd been expelled? "Never you mind," she evaded. "After all, it *is* Christmas, with a wedding to boot. Let's go home. We mustn't keep Sarah — and Solita — waiting." She took the bull by the horns and boldly marched over to Seth. "I apologize for my brother," she said with what little dignity she could muster. "His sense of humor is —"

"Don't fret yourself, Miss Sterling. Brothers are like that. Just ask Sarah." An unreadable expression lurked in Seth's eyes.

Dori felt a river of hot blood stream into her face, and she silently climbed into the waiting carriage. Seth obviously hadn't given a second thought to the comment that had caused her so much mortification. His response had been perfectly courteous, but Dori felt like a child who had been patted on the head and told to go play.

Torn between chagrin and resentment, Dori remained silent most of the way to the Diamond S, despite Matt's attempts to include her in the conversation. *What difference does it make what Seth thinks?* she asked herself. *He's just another cowhand on my brother's ranch.* Yet her innate honesty forced her to admit it did make a difference — a huge difference, and one she couldn't explain.

It seemed to Dori's disturbed mind as if

they would never reach the ranch. By the time they pulled in, the western sky was a study in reds and purples. Dori caught her breath. No Boston sunset could compare with this. She climbed from the carriage and gazed at the sprawling, hacienda-style ranch house, its white stucco walls rosy from the kiss of the setting sun. Light streamed from every window and from the open front door, welcoming Dori home. Two women waited on the wide front porch. One hurried to the top of the steps and met Dori's headlong rush with open arms.

"*Querida.* Dios be praised. You are home." Solita folded Dori into a tight embrace.

The familiar endearment changed Dori into a small girl, safe and secure in Solita's arms. Worn and weary from life in Boston followed by the fearsome experience of being trapped in the blizzard, she laid her head on the diminutive housekeeper's shoulder and let her tears fall.

Solita patted her shoulder and crooned, "Don't cry, little one. You are home and safe. Now you must meet Señorita Sarah, who has waited for your coming."

"Welcome home, sister," a musical voice said.

Dori freed herself from Solita's embrace and turned. A smiling replica of Seth stood

90

with both hands outstretched. The shy appeal in the young woman's wistful blue eyes showed the same anxiety Dori had felt about meeting Sarah. All Dori's preconceived notions vanished. Unless badly mistaken, she'd been as wrong about Sarah as about Seth.

Dori managed a shaky laugh and clasped Sarah's hands. "I'm so glad to meet you." It was true. The identical feeling she'd experienced when meeting Seth flowed through her. *What is it about the Andersons that calls to something deep inside me?* Dori wondered. *The goodness that Matt raved about?* She sighed. She was just too tired to figure it out.

The evening passed in a blur. Dori's mental turnaround concerning Seth and Sarah had left her feeling bewildered. Yet certainty that her brother was in no danger from either of them filled Dori with relief. She sank into her soft bed and murmured, "Thank You, God, for bringing me safely home." She burrowed farther down under the covers. "Please don't let anyone find out until after the honeymoon that I won't be going back to Boston." A few moments later, she fell into the soundest sleep she'd known since she left the Diamond S. Except for the Andersons' presence, it seemed like nothing had changed, after all.

The few days before Christmas fled like shadows before the rising sun. On Christmas morning Dori awoke to the shrill whinny of a horse. She ran to her window and looked outside. Curly, Bud, and Slim were standing by the prettiest pinto mare Dori had ever seen. Seth was in the saddle, patting the horse's neck. Curly's voice floated up to Dori.

"You are one lucky cuss, Seth. Miss Dori's gonna hug your neck when she sees Splotches."

Bud and Slim guffawed.

Dori felt herself turn scarlet. What did Curly mean? Had Seth Anderson bought her a horse? She thrilled to the idea even while knowing it was impossible and watched Seth slide to the ground. How would he answer Curly?

Seth just laughed. "Naw. It's her brother who's gonna get hugged. I just broke the mare." Splotches nosed him. "Hope she likes you, girl. If she doesn't, she's a mighty poor judge of horseflesh."

Like the pinto? Dori already loved her. She scrambled into her old riding clothes and pelted down the stairs and out to the corral, where Matt had joined the others. "Is she for me?" she burst out.

Matt raised one eyebrow. "What makes you think that? Do you deserve her?"

Dori's joy fled. She shifted uneasily but didn't flinch from Matt's probing gaze. Honesty forced her to admit, "No, but I love Splotches."

The cowboys went into spasms of laughter.

Matt took the reins from Seth and held them out to Dori. "Good enough. Merry Christmas, sister."

Excitement filled Dori. "A brand-new horse!" She threw her arms around Matt, then around the mare's neck. Splotches whickered and stamped one foot. Dori took the reins and swung into the saddle. "Thank you. She's gorgeous."

"She's also gentle. Seth broke her for you," Bud put in.

"Thank you, Seth."

Slim added before Seth could reply. "Aw, 'twasn't nothin'. Seth said Splotches was the easiest horse he ever broke. Say, ain't you gonna try her out?"

"You bet I am." Dori touched the pinto's sides with her boot heels and called over her shoulder, "I hope I can still ride western."

Splotches took off like a startled jackrabbit, followed by Curly's bellow, "Can she

93

still ride? I'll tell the world she can." A chorus of approving cowboy yells warmed Dori through and through.

She didn't head for home until the sun was high in the sky and her growling stomach clamored for the breakfast she had skipped. "Fine thing, running off on Christmas morning," she told her new horse. "But it was worth it." She reached the ranch and burst into the kitchen. "I'm starving."

Solita stopped tossing tortillas and smiled at Sarah, who was seated at the table with a cup of delicious-smelling Mexican cocoa that made Dori's mouth water. "You haven't changed."

Sarah laughed. "I don't wonder that you're hungry. You've been gone for hours."

"I lost track of time."

"I don't blame you. When I'm on a horse, I forget everything else. Riding gives me a sense of freedom." She stood. "Speaking of freedom, I'll still be a free woman tomorrow if I don't hustle. If you'll excuse me, I have to do some packing. After all, I'm marrying the most wonderful man in the world just a few hours from now."

If Dori hadn't already been won over by Sarah's integrity, the bride-to-be's expression would have settled all doubts. "Is there anything I can do to help you?"

"Feed that mountain lion raging inside you," Sarah advised. Her eyes twinkled. "One other thing. I like your riding outfit, but you might want to change for the wedding." A trill of laughter floated back as she ran out of the kitchen.

Dori had barely finished eating when Matt burst in. "Where's my girl — I mean, my other girl?" he wanted to know.

"Getting ready to become your wife," Dori told him.

"Yes." A poignant light came into his blue eyes. "Little sister, this is the happiest day of my life. I just pray that one day you will feel the way I do right now. Sarah completes my life."

As I once did.

Dori felt a twinge of regret for days that were gone forever, but it soon passed. No one in her right mind could be jealous of Sarah. Even in the few days Dori had been home she'd observed the way Matt and Sarah fit together like two blades on a fine pair of scissors. They would have a good life.

Dori swallowed hard. Would Matt's prayer for her be answered? Would she one day be readying herself to marry someone who would make her life complete? Someone as fine as her brother — someone she considered the most wonderful man in the world?

Dori wasn't the only one thinking about a life companion. While Seth waited to walk Sarah down the aisle of the Madera church, a pang of envy knocked at his heart's door. *God, do You have a girl like Sarah picked out for me?* He put aside the thought. Christmas and the wedding were making him soft. If God had someone in mind, He wasn't telling . . . and wouldn't until the time was right.

Seth grinned to himself and told Sarah, "You don't want to keep Matt waiting."

She nudged him and sent a pointed glance toward Dori, seated in the front row with Solita. "Just remember: Your turn's coming."

Seth felt his pulse quicken. He took revenge by whispering, "Naw. She's too Bostonish for a poor, lonesome cowpoke," and tried to ignore his poor, lonesome cowpoke's heartbeat that had changed from a slow walk to a full gallop.

ELEVEN

For the next few days, Dori reveled in her freedom. Despite Solita's protests, she rode Splotches when and where she chose. She teased Brett Owen until the foreman told her she was wilder than an unbroken mustang. Dori just laughed, pulled his Stetson down over his eyes, and danced away. Yet beneath her enjoyment, the guilty secret she carried stabbed at her conscience. Matt and Sarah would be home from their San Francisco honeymoon soon. What would they say when they learned Dori wasn't going back to Boston?

The morning of their scheduled return, Dori followed the tantalizing tang of good food down the staircase and through the open hall door into the sunny Diamond S kitchen. "What smells so good? I'm starved." She plunked down at the table.

"*Huevos rancheros.*" Solita set a plateful of

steaming fried eggs with chili sauce in front of Dori and added warm tortillas. Her white teeth gleamed in a broad smile. "The Brookside Finishing School for Young Ladies did not serve such food, no?"

Dori grinned. "Hardly. It was mush, mush, mush for breakfast. If I never see another bowl of oatmeal it will be too soon." She lifted a forkful of the mixture, blew on it to cool it down, and put it in her mouth. "Mmm. Better than I remember."

Solita beamed. "In a few months, you will be here in our casa for good. I promise you will never have to eat mush again."

The huevos rancheros suddenly lost all their taste. Before nightfall, Dori would have to confess she was already home for good. A letter from Miss Brookings lay on the desk in Matt's office. Dori's fingers itched to burn it before he and Sarah came, but knew she couldn't. She was already in enough trouble.

Dori sighed. She hated to spoil her brother's homecoming, but she just had to tell him before he saw the letter. She couldn't afford to have Matt read the Babbling Brook's recital of the events leading to her dismissal before he heard Dori's side of the story.

"I thought you were starving."

Solita's reminder yanked Dori back into the present. "I'm waiting for it to cool." She glanced at the counters laden with flour, sugar, spices, and a dozen large bowls and baking pans. "Are you planning to feed an army instead of Matt and Sarah, or are you going to open a bakery?"

Solita shook her head and her dark eyes glistened. "There must be pies and cakes and cookies for the shivaree. Señor Mateo and Señora Sarah escaped being troubled on their wedding night by staying at the Yosemite Hotel." She rolled her expressive eyes. "Even the most daring vaqueros would not dare holler and beat on pans outside the hotel until invited in for treats." She shrugged. "Tonight they will come here so we must be prepared."

Dori's heart sank. Shivarees were always fun, but being invaded by a horde of well-wishers on this particular night meant she would have no chance to confess. It was more than she could stand. She looked into Solita's kindly face and blurted out, "Solita, I'm in terrible trouble."

The housekeeper stared at her. "Señorita, how can this be? Dios be praised. He brought you safely home to us."

Dori drew in a great breath. "He did, Solita, but I'm not going back to school."

99

An icy voice spoke from the doorway leading into the great hall. "Begging your pardon, Miss Sterling, but you are going back. Haven't you caused your brother enough trouble without kicking up a fuss and refusing to finish the course you insisted on taking?"

Dori spun out of her chair so quickly it crashed to the floor. Her unflinching gaze bored into Seth's blazing blue eyes. She tried twice before she could hurl words at the glowering cowboy. "This is a private conversation, Mr. Eavesdropper. It doesn't concern you in the least."

"That's what you think," Seth shot back. "Sarah is my sister. She has a right to be happy. Anything that disturbs Matt affects her." He shook a finger in Dori's face. "Nothing is going to spoil their lives, get that? You're going to be on that train the day after tomorrow as scheduled." He paused and added, "You're going if I have to tie you on Splotches and wait at the station until I see the train leave."

Seth's words *spoil their lives* did what no amount or ranting or raving could do. Dori threw herself into Solita's arms and wailed, "I can't go back. I've been expelled."

An ominous silence pervaded the kitchen, broken only by Solita's gasp and Dori's hard breathing. Then Seth demanded, "What did you do this time?"

The scorn in his voice helped Dori gather her wits. "Nothing." She jerked free from Solita's embrace and glared at Seth. "I didn't do anything. How would you like being called a shameless hussy and accused of coquetting with the headmistress's nephew in a brazen attempt to weasel your way into society?" Memory heightened Dori's fury.

"What would you do if you were insulted and humiliated? An insufferable Englishman named Stancel Worthington III announced that he was going to civilize and marry me. His aunt said it would be over her dead body."

Seth's lips twitched. "Never having been a young lady, I can't really say. I'd sure be put out at being called names, but . . ." To Dori's amazement Seth threw his head back and roared. "If I were a girl — a young lady — and anyone with the moniker 'Stancel Worthington III' tried to lasso me, I'd tell him *adios* in a hurry."

The blood that had been furiously rushing through Dori's veins slowed, and she simmered down. "I did, but not before giving it to the Babbling Brook and 'dear Stancel' with both barrels." She felt her lips tilt in a grin.

"So she kicked you out of her precious school."

"Yes." Dori drooped. "She told me to never darken the door of her ladies' academy again. I skedaddled out of there as quick as I could." Dori spread her hands wide and she choked back tears. "I don't want to spoil Matt and Sarah's life, but I can't go back. Miss Brookings was so furious that all the gold in California during the gold rush can't buy my way back into the school."

"Matt doesn't know." The quiet finality of Seth's comment sent misery flooding through Dori.

"No. I couldn't say anything before the wedding and ruin the happiest day of his life."

Solita stood as if frozen. Seth took a deep breath, expelled it in a long sigh, and advised, "Don't tell Matt and Sarah today. Tomorrow will be time enough."

It suddenly seemed tremendously important for Dori to know what Seth was thinking. She took a step nearer and implored, "You don't believe I was wrong, do you?"

His face went blank, as if he'd pulled down a shade and turned an OPEN sign to CLOSED. "Not this time, Miss Sterling." He stalked out, leaving Dori smarting from his subtle references to her past behavior.

She crossed to the table and sank back in a chair. "Well, just when I thought Mr. Know-It-All was beginning to thaw, he closes up like an oyster. Doesn't he like girls, or is it just me?" The thought hurt.

Solita's round brown eyes opened wide. "Señor Seth likes señoritas, but not as much as they like him."

"I'll bet they do," Dori muttered.

"Sí. He could court many of them if he had time." She smiled and looked wise. "Especially Señorita Sheridan."

An unreasonable pang of jealousy flowed through Dori. "You mean Sarah's friend Abby, from the Yosemite Hotel?" *Why should you care?* a little voice whispered. *He is nothing to you.* Why then, did she hold her breath and wait for the reply?

Solita nodded. "When she comes to visit, her dark eyes look at Seth, and she blushes."

Dori clenched her hands under the table. "What does he do?"

Solita reached for a large bowl and measured flour into it. "Señor Seth teases her, the same as Curly, Bud, and Slim do. They are all glad when she comes."

That explains it, Dori thought. *No wonder Seth has no use for me. Abby is probably the perfect little lady who would never dream of doing the things I do.* Much as Dori wanted to deny it, ever since she'd met Seth at the station, she'd hoped to find favor with the tall cowboy. Brief encounters during the last few days had whetted her desire to get to know him better, but in vain. Until today, anywhere she was he usually wasn't.

The imp of mischief that lurked on Dori's shoulder, poised and ready to take off, sprang to life. She would make Seth Anderson like her. She would show him that she was more than an irresponsible nuisance.

How? Seth's curt "not this time" clearly showed his sympathy for her present plight wasn't enough to tip the scales in her favor. *If only I could do something worthwhile, something noble and selfless and grown-up. I can start by giving up this morning's ride and help Solita with the baking. It isn't much, and Seth probably won't even notice, but maybe I can think of something else while I work.*

"It feels good to be in the kitchen," Dori told Solita while they chattered away and filled the kitchen with rows and rows of baked goods. "Finishing schools don't train young ladies to cook. Just to be young ladies." She bit into a warm cookie and mumbled, "I suppose you and Sarah spend a lot of time here."

"Sí." Solita deftly trimmed excess pie

crust off an apple pie and cut designs in the top with a sharp knife. "We also teach the Mexican children to speak English." A ripple of laughter set her shoulders shaking. "The señoras, too."

A tingle started at Dori's toes and moved upward. Such a worthwhile undertaking might make Seth sit up and take notice. "Do you think I can help?"

The skepticism on Solita's face wasn't very flattering. Neither were her raised eyebrows, but she only said, "We shall see." She rolled out another pie crust. "If you begin, you must come each time and not disappoint the students."

"I will." *If it kills me.* Dori felt a twinge for what would mean lost riding time. Was such a commitment really worth it, just to impress Seth? She smiled to herself. Right now, she wanted his approval so much she would do just about anything to get it. Besides, working with Solita and Sarah would give her time to get better acquainted with her new sister-in-law — and through her, learn what made Seth Anderson tick.

Dori and Solita had barely finished the baking and gotten supper underway when a laughing Matt and Sarah arrived. As Dori feared, there was no time for confessions. At supper, the newlyweds bubbled over with tales of San Francisco: the trip across San Francisco Bay, with icy waves attacking the ferry. The multitude of tall buildings. The salty smell from the seemingly endless Pacific Ocean. The hustle and bustle of carriages and horse-drawn carts. The steep hills and cable cars. The Chinese theater.

"Showing Sarah the wonders of San Francisco was like seeing it through new eyes," Matt told them with a sly look at his bride.

Sarah's eyes shone with love. "It was exciting and interesting, but I was glad to shake the dust of San Francisco off my shoes and come home. I don't like cities. Madera is big enough for me."

It was the perfect opening for Dori's not-so-gladsome news, but her throat dried, and her tongue cleaved to the roof of her mouth. Now was not the time to confess she had shaken the dust of Boston off her shoes. Yet she had never felt more miserable and alone than during the shivaree.

Even Solita's unspoken sympathy couldn't lift Dori's spirits. Standing to one side while the others made merry, Dori thought of her conductor friend on the journey home, and of the story she had told him. The sword of Damocles had fallen on her in Boston, but Dori suspected the real damage was yet to come.

The jovial crowd finally left. All was quiet. Seth had said good night and gone out, leaving Matt, Sarah, and Dori alone in the great room. He banked the fire and told his bride, "Go on up. I'll just have a quick look at the mail and be right with you."

Dori froze with one foot on the bottom stair. "No! I mean, why tonight? Surely there's nothing that can't wait until morning."

"I agree." Sarah linked her arm in her husband's, but Matt's gaze never left Dori. It made her feel like a butterfly on a pin. Why did he have to know her so well?

"You seem mighty concerned." He cocked an eyebrow. "What have you been up to now?"

Every resolution to wait fled. Dori sank to the bottom stair, buried her face in her hands, and said, "I've been dismissed."

"Dismissed? Dismissed from what?" Matt demanded.

Dori licked her dry lips. "Expelled. Kicked out. I can't go back to Brookside — ever."

TWELVE

Hot tears burned behind Dori's aching eyelids. She kept her head down, unable to face Matt, Sarah, and the accumulation of sins that had led to her being banished from Brookside. *Forgive me, God, and please let Matt and Sarah forgive me.* Her heart added what her mind refused to ask: *Seth, too.*

Matt's voice sliced into the quiet room like a sharp knife. "You had better explain yourself, Dolores."

Dori flinched. Matt only called her by her full name when she was in trouble. She raised her head and looked into his set face. "It . . . it wasn't my fault, Matt." The skeptical look in his eyes hurt her even more than the disappointment she saw. "You know I don't lie."

She got up from the bottom stair and clasped her hands behind her back. "I did a lot of things that should have gotten me expelled, but this time, I wasn't to blame. If

Miss Brookings's nephew hadn't come from England, I'd still be at school. He was trouble from the minute I almost knocked him out the front door and —"

"Up to your old tricks, I see."

"Not this time. He just happened to be in the way." Dori quickly related her trials and tribulations with Stancel Worthington III. "He was impossible. If you ever met him, you'd know what I mean."

"Spare me the lurid details."

"I can't." Dori told how she was called on the carpet, insulted by the headmistress, and ordered to leave Brookside posthaste. She ended with, "Even if I *could* go back, would you want me to after being called hussy and brazen? I'll bet Miss Brookings didn't put *that* in the letter on your desk."

A muscle twitched in Matt's cheek. "Why don't we see?" He grabbed the letter, opened it, and read aloud. " 'Mr. Sterling, your sister Dolores is no longer welcome at my school. I have been patient and long-suffering in order to abide by your wishes and keep her here. She, however, has been a disturbing element ever since she arrived. She should have been sent home long ago. In any event, her latest transgression cannot be overlooked.

" 'Dolores set her cap for my dear nephew

Stancel the moment he arrived. In order to attract his attention, she slid down the banister rail — which is strictly prohibited — and boldly pursued him at every opportunity. Stancel clearly showed his preference for Gretchen van Dyke, but Dolores wove an evil spell around him. She so enmeshed him in her wiles that Stancel actually considered civilizing, then marrying her.' "

A muffled snicker from Sarah, who had kept silent all through Matt and Dori's conversation, halted Matt's reading. Dori gaped at her. Sarah had both hands over her mouth. Her face was redder than the last embers in the fireplace. "Sorry," she apologized, tears streaming. "It's just that no one in real life says 'wove an evil spell,' or 'enmeshed him in her wiles.' Dori, your headmistress must have been reading dime novels on the sly."

Dori sent Sarah a look of approval. She turned to Matt and caught a flicker of his bride's contagious amusement cross his face before he said, "Let's have the rest of it. 'I do believe Dolores actually thought Stancel's temporary aberration would gain her an entrance into a level of society she could achieve in no other way. When she discovered I would not stand for it, Dolores called

110

dear Stancel all kinds of barnyard names that plainly showed her lack of breeding.

" 'Now that this unspeakable trouble-maker is out of the way, Stancel will naturally seek someone eminently more suitable than the uncivilized sister of a keeper of gentleman cows.' "

Matt paused. The flicker of amusement grew into a blaze. A chuckle escaped. "Gentleman cows? I wonder where she got that. 'As you know, Mr. Sterling, there is no monetary refund for those who do not complete their schooling, unless there is serious illness. I commend Dolores back into your keeping, and may God have mercy on your soul.' "

Matt threw the letter aside and looked at Sarah, then Dori. His lips broadened into a grin. "You notice I am no longer 'dear Mr. Sterling.' " A belly laugh followed. "So it's hail-and-farewell to Brookside Finishing School for Young Ladies."

Dori ran across the room and threw her arms around him. Was this how Christian, the hero in *The Pilgrim's Progress,* felt when the heavy burdens he carried on his journey from the City of Destruction to the Celestial City finally dropped away? Dori wanted to skip, leap, and shout. If Matt could laugh like this, surely she wasn't in too much hot water. His arms closed around her. Dori sighed with relief. Let Miss Brookings and her pompous nephew go hang. Miss Dori Sterling was home, safe, and forgiven.

Dori's joy was short-lived. All too soon, Matt removed her clinging arms from around his waist and dropped his hands on her shoulders. Every trace of amusement had vanished. "I can't condone Miss Brookings's behavior," he said quietly, "but neither are you blameless. You've been taught since childhood that actions have consequences. There's always a day of reckoning."

Dori shivered in spite of the warm room. "What are you going to do with me?"

"I don't know yet. Drastic circumstances call for drastic measures."

Dori's heart plummeted to her toes. This was not good.

Sarah's soft voice brought the dialogue to a standstill. "It's late, and I'm sure we're all tired, Matt. Suppose you and Dori continue this conversation tomorrow."

Dori could have hugged her. The journey from confession through hilarity to facing an unknown future had taken its toll. Her energy was at such a low ebb she wondered if she could make it up the stairs to her room. "Good night, Sarah. Good night, Matt." She grasped the rail of the staircase and began to climb, too tired to worry over what tomorrow might bring.

After a restless, nightmare-filled night, Dori slept long past the usual rising hour for the Diamond S. When she came downstairs, she found Solita and Sarah at the kitchen table, steaming cups of coffee before them.

"Did you sleep well?" Sarah asked. Concern shadowed her voice.

"No. Do you know what Matt is going to do?"

Sarah shook her head. "I'm not sure he knows. We didn't discuss it last night."

Dori stared out the window into a sunny day. The sound of stamping hooves and a whinny from the corral chirked her up a bit. "Where's Matt?"

"Right here." He stepped into the kitchen. "How about a second cup of coffee, Solita?"

How can he look so rested and free from worry? Dori resentfully wondered. "So what's the verdict?" She hated herself for sounding flippant but couldn't stand one minute more of not knowing what lay in store for her.

"Do you want Solita and me to leave?"

Sarah asked.

"Please stay," Dori said. "You can be the jury when Judge Sterling pronounces sentence on the accused. Maybe you will plead for mercy on my behalf."

"That attitude won't help you," Matt stated. He accepted the coffee from Solita, waited until she sat down again, then seated himself in a chair beside Sarah. "You're eighteen years old. Too old to think you can rule the roost, act as you please without regard for others, and not be held accountable."

Dori wilted. This was worse than she'd expected, especially when Matt's reception of Miss Brookings's letter had brought hope for a lesser scolding.

"First of all, you are going to finish your last term of schooling. Just because you aren't going back to Brookside doesn't mean you can run wild on the ranch."

Stunned, Dori clenched her fingers until the nails bit into the palms of her hands. "I can't go back to school in Madera. I'm older than everyone there. They'll ask why I didn't stay in Boston." The thought of being humiliated lent Dori the courage to continue. "Please, Matt, don't make me do that. I'll never live down being kicked out of Brookside."

"You've lived down other things," Matt reminded her.

"Not like this." Dori shook her head until her black curls flew every which way. "It will be the ruination of me. Besides, only you three and Seth know why I'm not going back. Can't we keep it that way?"

Matt drummed his fingers on the table. "You do have a point, but . . ."

Sarah placed one hand over her husband's. A glow filled her eyes. "Matt, I never had a chance for advanced schooling. Would you — could you hire a tutor to come to the ranch and teach both Dori and me? I feel so ignorant compared with you."

"Ignorant? You're the smartest person I know," Matt argued. "There's nothing you can't do, even teach the Mexicans to speak English."

"Pooh, Solita does most of the teaching," Sarah scoffed. "Besides, I don't mean ignorant about living, just about books and things."

Humbled by Sarah's frank admission of her shortcomings, Dori did likewise. "I know I don't deserve it, but having a tutor and studying with Sarah would be wonderful." She inwardly groaned at the thought of being cooped up doing lessons when Splotches and the entire great outdoors beckoned her. But it was better than having to tuck her tail between her legs and go back to school in Madera.

"The tutor will see to it that I make up what I'll be missing at Brookside," Dori added. *And it will not include ballroom dancing,* she silently vowed, wise enough to hold her tongue. She was already skating on the thinnest of ice.

Matt's brows drew together in a straight line. "So where am I to get a tutor? Any teacher worth his salt will already be teaching this time of year."

"Pray for one." Dori clapped her hand over her mouth. Had she really said that?

Matt looked astonished. So did Sarah and Solita.

"I'm serious," Dori told them, surprised to discover it was true. "Doesn't the Bible tell us that if we ask, we shall receive?" Laughter bubbled out. "And if we seek, we shall find? Well, you need to seek a tutor."

Matt tilted back in his chair and clasped his hands behind his head. "It never ceases to amaze me how you can quote scripture when it's to your benefit, sister dear. I have to admit, though, it's a good idea." He stretched. "Now if this discussion is over, I have work to do." He stood, leaned down and kissed Sarah, and strode out.

"Dios will surely help Señor Mateo find the right person," Solita observed. She smiled at Dori. "I will make your breakfast now."

"Can I help?"

"No. You sit and talk with Señora Sarah." The housekeeper disappeared into the pantry.

The postponement of Dori's day of reckoning released her mischievous spirit. While Solita was out of the kitchen, Dori whispered to Sarah, "I wonder what kind of tutor God will send?"

Sarah laughed and patted her hand. "Who knows? God has such a sense of humor He will probably surprise us. Maybe even shock us."

"I just hope the tutor has a sense of humor," Dori flashed back. "If he's anything like 'dear Stancel,' we're sunk."

For several days, it appeared there were no unemployed tutors anywhere near Madera. Dori conscientiously made it a matter of prayer, but when time went by with no success, despair set in. If no tutor could be found, she was doomed to return to school in Madera. She intensified her prayers.

Two full weeks after her return to the Diamond S, the tutor arrived. When the sound of buggy wheels halted in front of

117

the wide front porch, Dori and Sarah rushed out. Sarah giggled. She pinched Dori's arm and said, "I told you God might shock us. Now we'll see if He has."

Matt helped someone from the buggy. "Sarah, Dori, meet Miss Katie O'Riley, your new tutor."

"I'm actually for bein' a teacher and a governess," Katie said.

Dori's jaw dropped. Her new "tutor" had the reddest hair, the greenest eyes, and the most freckles on her tip-tilted nose that Dori had ever seen. She looked to be only a few years older than Dori and her accent was pure, lilting Irish when she said, "So you're for bein' Mrs. Sarah and Miss Dolores. Mercy me, but you're two fine colleens." A trill of laughter set Katie's eyes asparkle. And as Dori's grandmother used to say, "It warmed the very cockles of a body's heart."

Thank You, God, Dori breathed — and stepped forward to welcome Katie O'Riley.

THIRTEEN

"Whoa, Copper."

Late one Saturday afternoon, Seth Anderson reined in his sorrel gelding just outside the corral and wearily slid from the saddle. He'd been riding the range, looking for a small bunch of cattle that were either lost, strayed, or stolen — most likely stolen — without success. He glanced toward the ranch house. An assortment of riderless horses and a couple of buggies littered the front yard.

Seth scowled. His earlier predictions about life on the Diamond S never being the same once Dori Sterling turned up had been fulfilled. The coming of Katie O'Riley had added to the problem. With two attractive, unmarried females on hand, single and widowed men for miles around flocked to the ranch like honeybees to a clover field.

Seth snorted. "A bunch of lovesick pups, as far as I'm concerned. I've never seen so many duded-up visitors or smelled so much hair tonic. I can't tell yet how Katie feels about all this masculine attention, but anyone who isn't blind can see that Dori glories in it. She holds court as if every male age eighteen and over is her private property."

Seth unsaddled Copper and continued to grumble while he rubbed the sorrel down. "You're the best listener on the ranch," he said. Copper whinnied and nudged his soft nose against Seth's shoulder as if to agree. His master went on with his complaints.

"Curly, Bud, Slim, and most of the outfit are just as bad. In all my born days I never heard such a passel of excuses for laying off work. Curly's had more bellyaches lately than in all the time I've been here. Bud can't ride 'cause his 'rheumatics' — whatever that is — are acting up."

Seth groomed Copper until he shone brighter than his name. "Slim takes the cake. I heard him tell Brett this morning that he reckoned he was just 'too tuckered out to chase rustlers or cow-type critters today.' Matt's gotta do something and do it pronto, or we may as well kiss the rest of the herd good-bye."

Disgusted and discouraged, Seth turned Copper loose in the pasture, got himself slicked up, and went to find Sarah. Maybe she could do something with Dori. To his amazement, he got little sympathy.

"Dori is still young, even though she's eighteen," Sarah told him over coffee in the kitchen. "Of course she has the bit in her teeth. She's been penned up at school for two years. Although she won't admit it, I suspect she hated every minute there but was too proud to come home. Don't let her get under your skin, Seth. She'll settle down." Sarah smiled at him. "Katie is good for her. Even in the short time she's been with us, she's been rubbing off on Dori."

A merry laugh floated through the open hall door and into the kitchen. "From what I can see, it's the other way around," Seth growled. "Sounds like Dori has Katie wrapped around her little finger."

Sarah shook her head. "Don't you believe it. Our Irish colleen is full of fun, but she's a strict disciplinarian in the classroom. If Dori or I don't have our lessons prepared to her satisfaction, she looks at us with those big emerald eyes and says, 'You'll be for doin' this over — as many times as it takes for it to be done right and proper.' "

Sarah's imitation of the new teacher brought a grin to Seth's face. "I'm glad to see there's someone on this ranch who Dori can't push around. I would have thought she'd pitch a fit at having to be taught."

"I'm sure she'd like to, but the alternative is spending spring term at school in Madera." His sister raised one eyebrow and smirked. "By the way, I'd say there are two someone's here on the ranch who Dori can't push around." Before Seth could answer, Sarah changed the subject. "Matt says there's going to be a barn raising soon, followed by a barn dance. Are you taking anyone?"

Feeling he had been bested concerning Dori, Seth was in no mood for frolicking. "Probably not."

"How about Abby?" Mischief lurked in Sarah's blue eyes.

Seth stood and glared down at her. "As Katie would say, 'Don't you be for matchmaking.' It beats all that when folks get married, all they can think of is getting everyone else hitched up."

"So do you plan on spending your life in single blessedness?" Sarah teased.

"Better single blessedness than double cursedness," Seth retorted. He got up and stalked toward the kitchen door, pursued by his sister's mocking laughter. A moment later, her soft voice halted him.

"I'm sorry, Seth. Matt and I are so happy.

I want you to be, too." Her voice trembled.

Repentant for acting so cussed, Seth spun around. "I know. It's just that I won't marry until God sends the right girl and lets me know she is the right one. Stepping into double harness any other way is asking for a heap of trouble."

Sarah flew to his side and hugged him. "Maybe He has already sent the right one."

Seth blinked. Why should her remark set a vision of a dark-haired young woman in a velvet cloak as blue as her eyes dancing in his mind? His heartbeat quickened. "What do you mean?"

Sarah looked innocent. "You've paid attention to Abby, and she's a good Christian girl. You like her, don't you?"

Seth felt his muscles relax. "Sure. She's pretty and fun." He bent a stern gaze on Sarah. "Just don't get ideas in that head of yours. Save the room for 'book-larnin,' as Curly calls it." He tweaked the red-gold braid wrapped around Sarah's head. But she had the last word.

"Why don't you invite Dori to the barn raising and the dance?"

With a mumbled protest against females, matchmaking sisters in particular, Seth fled. But the suggestion Sarah had planted in his mind took root. Half the countryside would be on hand to help replace the barn on the Rocking R that had caught fire and burned to the ground a few weeks earlier. Seth would be the envy of Madera if he took Dori to the raising.

How ridiculous to even consider such an idea. "Escorting a young lady in order to show off is not fit behavior, God," he prayed. "Help me stay true to Your teachings and 'do unto others.' I sure wouldn't want anyone to show up at a barn raising with me just to make other folks sit up and take notice." Yet a feeling of regret nagged at him. If Dori were as innocent and good as she appeared, what a wife she would make. Seth sighed. Since she wasn't, he would continue to keep his distance and not subject himself to her charm.

Fate and Matt Sterling tossed Seth's carefully laid plans to the four winds. After Dori sneaked away from her studies for the second time and took off on Splotches, Matt sought out Seth. "Ride with me, will you?"

"Sure." Seth laid aside the currycomb with which he'd been grooming Copper. The grim expression in his boss's eyes warned of trouble.

Matt lost no time in confirming Seth's suspicions. Once Copper and Matt's buckskin, Chase, swung into an easy canter, Matt abruptly said, "You know what 'fightin' wages' are, don't you?"

What on earth? The feeling that rough water lay ahead made Seth wary. "Of course. Extra pay for hands who fight rustlers and other dangers."

"I have a proposition for you. I'd hoped Dori would settle down. She hasn't." Matt spit the words out like bullets. "It's bad enough having a herd of lovesick boys and men, including a couple bad eggs from town, hanging around all the time. What's worse is that Dori believes she can ride as well as she did two years ago. She can't, and she's pushing Splotches too hard and too fast. I caught her trying to jump a fence the other day after I told her not to. The pinto hesitated long enough to break her stride, then nicked the top rail and took a nasty fall. Dori sailed over Splotches' head. If it had been hardpan ground instead of pastureland, they could both have been badly hurt."

A brooding look crept into Matt's eyes. "What worries me most is that Dori is bound and determined to ride every horse on the ranch, even the mustangs that haven't been broken."

Pity for his boss and friend shot through Seth, but he remained silent. After a long moment, Matt continued. "This is no way to start married life. I need to be with Sarah, not keeping track of my sister twenty-four hours of the day. Seth, if you'll take over for me, I'll up your pay to fightin' wages."

Had the sky opened and sent a thunderbolt down on Seth, he couldn't have been more shocked. "Me ride herd on Dori? Excuse me, Boss, but you must be out of your mind. Rustlers are one thing. Your sister is a heap worse."

"I know it's a lot to ask, but I'm desperate," Matt confessed. "In addition to disrupting my schedule and driving me to the point where I'm about ready to fire the entire outfit, Dori is rapidly becoming the talk of Madera because she likes being popular and doesn't care who knows it." He sighed. "I'd hoped her narrow escape from being trapped on the train home from Boston would curb her high spirits. Or that making her study would help. Katie O'Riley is doing her best, but she can't compete with this." He waved across the flat land that rolled away to the foothills, with the snow-capped Sierra Nevada in the distance.

Unwilling sympathy caused Seth to say, "I can understand that." He found himself repeating what Sarah had said. "After all,

Dori has been cooped up and away from all this for a long time."

"I know, but she needs to learn self-control. That's where you come in."

Another ripple of shock went through Seth. He'd rather wrestle ornery cattle than be responsible for the wild girl. Besides, in spite of his scorn, he secretly admitted a powerful attraction hid deep inside him. It would be downright dangerous for him to spend the time in Dori's company that would be necessary should he agree to Matt's outlandish proposition. "I —"

Matt cut him off. "Wait until you hear what I have in mind. Before Dori went to Boston, she was a fine rider. Like I said, the trouble is, she thinks she's as good as ever. On the surface she is. However, two years of occasional sidesaddle rides on Boston trotting paths have undermined her ability. She needs to restore the range skills you and I know are necessary to live here. This land is beautiful; it can also be harsh and unforgiving. Varmints both two- and four-legged roam the range. Splotches is a great horse, but she's still young and relatively untried."

A poignant light came into Matt's troubled eyes. "Sarah and I would both feel better with Dori in your care. Take her out riding every day except Sunday. On school days, make it in the afternoon. Be sure Dori carries either a Colt .45 or a Winchester .73 carbine when she rides, and see to it that she can shoot as straight as a man. Teach her trick riding and roping, anything to hold her interest. If I know my dear sister — and I do — she will be on her mettle and determined to conquer whatever task you give her. Keep her at it, and wear her out until she's too tired to think up mischief."

Seth snorted. "Is that all?" Dislike for the idea warred with loyalty to Matt and the knowledge someone needed to take the high-spirited girl in hand.

Matt's keen eyes bored into him. Seth had the feeling the boss could read his mind. "It won't be easy," Matt warned. "I'd say it will pretty near be a full-time job. So what do you say?"

Seth didn't answer until they reached his favorite spot on the ranch, a place he had learned to love. The promontory that over-looked the ranch offered both privacy and beauty. The entire valley spread out below them, dotted with dark clumps of the vineyards and orchards that had sprung up north of the San Joaquin River. Diamond S cattle roamed the rolling rangeland that lay closer to their lookout.

Seth slid from Copper and let the reins hang to the ground. Matt swung from his saddle and did likewise. Unless something spooked them, the horses were trained to stand, so the men were in no danger of being left afoot. After a long silence, Matt quietly said, "Well?"

Seth squared his shoulders. How could he turn Matt down? He owed him more than he could ever repay. "I will do it on two conditions. First and most important, if I take charge of training Dori, I must be allowed to handle her in my own way. That means no matter what I do, you, Sarah, Brett, or anyone else can't interfere. If it's a problem, the deal's off." He took a deep breath and held it, torn between wishing Matt would argue and secretly hoping he wouldn't.

Matt's strong hand shot out and grabbed Seth's. "Agreed."

Seth's breath came out in a loud *whoosh*. "Second, no fightin' wages. My thirty dollars a month and keep are plenty."

"Doesn't seem right to me," Matt objected. "You'll be taking on a bigger job than any of the other hands."

Seth didn't give an inch. "Those are my terms. Think about it. If it ever got back to Dori that I was being paid for looking after her, she'd blow the whole thing sky-high."

Matt's heartfelt chortle signaled his relief. "You've got that right. When do you want to start?" He looked shamefaced. "Who should tell her? You or me?"

Seth ignored the tingling sensation of stepping from light into the dark unknown and nonchalantly said, "Might as well be me. If I'm going to boss her, she needs to know it right away. Just one thing. I have a feeling I'm not Dori's favorite person on the Diamond S. What if she turns me down flat?"

The grim expression that had disappeared with Seth's acceptance of the scheme returned. It boded no good for a wayward sister. "She won't. I promise you that." Matt leaped to Chase's saddle. "Let's go home. I can't wait to see Dori's face when she learns what we have in store for her."

Seth didn't reply. But on the long ride back to the ranch, he wondered. *Lord, what am I getting myself into? I'm going to need Your help and need it bad.*

FOURTEEN

" 'It was the best of times, it was the worst of times, it was the age of wisdom, it was the age of foolishness.' "

Dori flung the worn copy of *A Tale of Two Cities* to her desk in the Diamond S schoolroom and cast a longing glance out the window. A hint of frost glistened in the sunlight, and the whinny of horses in the corral was enough to drive her to distraction. "Studying about the French Revolution on a day like this is foolish," she grumbled. "Charles Dickens was wrong. Not being able to ride until afternoon is the 'worst of times.' " She slumped in her seat and silently dared her teacher or Sarah to challenge her.

Katie O'Riley's emerald eyes darkened. Her usually laughter-filled voice turned to ice. "You're for knowing nothing about the worst of times," she retorted.

Dori felt ashamed of her outburst but felt

compelled to defend herself. "It was the worst of times when I was in Boston. You can't imagine how bad —"

"Can't imagine?" Katie cut her off mid-sentence. She placed her hands on her hips, elbows akimbo, and tossed her red head. Every freckle stood out on her pink and white skin. "It's you who can't be for imagining what real hardship is. Hundreds of thousands of men, women, and children died from hunger during the Irish Potato Famine in the 1840s. Mother and Da nearly starved to death. For years they hoarded money to purchase passage to America, though 'twas sorely needed for food."

Dori's insides twisted at the pain in Katie's face. Her own face burned. How could she have been so insensitive? Whenever Katie was at repose, her usually merry face revealed a sadness that should have warned Dori that life had not always been easy for the Irish colleen. Yet caught up with herself, Dori hadn't known or cared about Katie's story.

Her teacher wasn't finished. Her eyes blazed and words poured out like water over a broken dam. "Conditions on the journey in those times were so unspeakable that the ships were called 'coffin boats.' If it hadn't been for the mercy of our heavenly Father,

Mother and Da would have been among the hundreds who died at sea. Even when they reached the 'Promised Land,' as America was said to be, their troubles weren't over. Irish 'micks' weren't welcome.

"I was born in a New York City tenement. Da worked on the docks. Mother took in washing. We were mocked and despised." Katie's lips trembled. "The hard work finished what the famine and terrible journey began. Mother and Da went home to heaven a few years back."

Sarah, who had remained quiet during Katie's story, gasped. "How did you live?"

Katie proudly raised her head. "Irish-women aren't for giving up. I hired myself out to a wealthy woman who was more interested in society doings than in her children. But I wanted more than being a nursemaid all my life. The master of the house had a great library. When he saw I hungered to learn, he told me to help myself to his books."

Enthralled by the story, Dori burst out, "How did you end up here?"

Some of the tension left Katie's pretty face. "The Father in heaven was surely looking out for me," she reverently said. "The master had business connections every-where. A little over a year ago, a man from

Fresno wrote asking if the master knew anyone capable of handling his three motherless daughters. I'd always wanted to see the West and agreed." She sighed. "All was for going well until the flood."

Dori straightened. The threat of winter flooding was a fact of life. This year, the Fancher, Red, and Big Dry creeks had surged into Fresno. Despite the townspeople's best efforts, the flood could not be controlled. It swept through town, tearing down hastily-constructed levees and leaving the streets under so much water folks had to be rescued by boat.

"Were you caught in the flood?" Dori breathlessly asked Katie.

She shook her curly red head. "No. But the worst-hit building was the schoolhouse. A foot-deep layer of mud covered the first floor. It will take weeks to repair. The master decided this was a good time to send his daughters to a school for young ladies in San Francisco for spring term."

"I hope they have better luck there than I did in Boston."

Katie's eyes twinkled for the first time since the conversation had taken a disastrous turn. "At least they are too young to interest an English dancing master," she teased. Dori groaned, but the next moment

Katie grew serious.

"The master asked to wed me, but I had no love for him, nor he for me. He was just for being kind." A look of awe crossed her expressive face. "I prayed to our Father in heaven, and a few days later, the master came in with news. He'd heard that a Mr. Matthew Sterling was looking for a teacher. Your brother came to Fresno and fetched me here." She added in a choky-sounding voice, "It's been like I found a home." Bright tears fell.

Dori couldn't speak, but Sarah quickly slipped her arm around Katie and said, "This is your home, Katie, for as long as you want to stay." Mischief filled her blue eyes. "I'm just not sure how long that will be. If my eyes don't deceive me, a certain young cowpuncher will have something to say about that."

Katie turned scarlet, but Dori's heart leaped to her throat. She stared at the two. Did Sarah mean . . . surely she couldn't think . . . was the young cowpuncher Seth? Just a little shorter than Matt, and not quite as broad-shouldered, Seth's crown of hair glowed as brightly as his sister's. It contrasted nicely with his richly tanned face and made his eyes look bluer than ever. Astride Copper, the cowboy was attractive enough to capture any girl's attention.

Confusion fell on Dori like a saddle blanket on Splotches. According to Solita, Seth had been keeping company with Abby Sheridan. Had he transferred his affections to Katie? Well, why not? Any man who won the Irish maiden's heart would be blessed.

Jealousy as green as Katie's plaid dress sped through Dori and battled with disgust for feeling that way. After what Katie had gone through, she deserved happiness. Unbidden, a prayer winged its way upward. *Please, just don't let it be with Seth. There are plenty of other single men to choose from.* A little voice inside mocked, *Then why don't* you *take one of them?*

Heat rushed to Dori's face. That was not a question she wanted to answer.

Reprieve came in the form of a knock on the schoolroom door and the sound of chattering. "Are you ladies finished in there?" Matt called. "The children are here for their lesson, and I need to see Dori."

Katie pulled away from Sarah. "Just a minute, please." She quickly crossed to Dori, who stood frozen. "Will you be for forgiving me for losing my temper?"

Dori shook her head. "You're the one who needs to forgive. I didn't know." She impulsively held out her hand. "Friends again?"

136

"Of course." Katie looked surprised. "Irish temper is like the wind. It comes without warning then is gone, *poof.*" She pressed Dori's hand and grinned. "Better run along and see what your brother wants."

"Wonder what I've done now?" Dori whispered. She stepped outside and blinked in the sunlight. Matt and Seth stood nearby, arms crossed and gazes fixed on her.

"Seth has something to say to you," Matt said. "I'll leave you to him, but before I go, you need to know I approve of everything he's going to tell you." He walked away, leaving Dori speechless and staring after him.

Dori's mouth fell open. What was Seth going to say to her that had her brother's approval? It didn't — it couldn't mean Seth had received permission from Matt to court her. *Don't be stupid,* she told herself, *There's Abby and Katie . . .* Dori's thoughts trailed off, but her traitorous heart taunted, *What else could it be?*

The tall cowboy doffed his Stetson. "If I may have your attention, Miss Sterling?"

The hint of sarcasm in his voice shattered the cocoon of silence that surrounded Dori. "Yes?" Her heart thumped.

"From now on, we'll be spending afternoons together," Seth told her.

137

"Together?"

"Yes." Seth raised one eyebrow. "I'll be in charge at all times. You'll do what I say, when I say it, and how."

Dori blinked. This didn't sound like a suitor eager to please. Rebellion rose, although Seth's masterful attitude intrigued her. "What if I don't?"

His measuring gaze never left her face. "Then the deal's off. Either I'm the boss, or Matt can get someone else to train you."

"Train me?" Her voice rose a full octave from its usual pitch. Did this . . . this oaf think he was going to train her to be his wife? She'd had enough of that with Stancel. "Train me for what?"

He looked surprised. "For fitting you with the skills you need to survive. Matt promised that you wouldn't turn me down."

If Dori hadn't been so angry she would have laughed in his face. Seth was even more insufferable than Stancel had been. As for Matt, she couldn't wait to tell him a thing or two.

"Matt wants me to turn you into the rider you used to be before going east." Anticipation sparkled in Seth eyes. "Roping, too, and trick riding, as well as shooting."

Thud! Dori's hopes of being courted crashed to the hard ground. She took a deep breath. Seth must never know what she had thought. *The best of times, the worst of times,* she thought bitterly. Another phrase from the story came to mind. *"The spring of hope, it was the winter of despair."* She had sprung from hope to despair in less time than it took to spring into a saddle.

Dori opened her mouth to blast Seth, to tell him he was the last person on the ranch she wanted to teach her anything. She paused. No. There was a better way. She would go along with his and Matt's scheme. She would learn everything he could teach her, then flaunt it by showing Seth she was as good or better than any hand on the range, including him.

Glee over her decision erased some of Dori's frustration. Long hours together would give her the opportunity to crack the wall of indifference she sensed in Seth when she was around. "So when do we start?"

"After dinner. I'll see that Splotches is saddled and ready."

Dori gritted her teeth at his nonchalance. She wanted to tell him she was perfectly capable of saddling her own horse but refrained. A small smile tilted her lips upward. She'd fooled Matt with her acting ability in Boston years ago. Surely she could hoodwink the brash cowboy who thought he could teach her skills she had possessed since childhood.

For the first few rides, Dori donned the docile attitude of a novice at the feet of a learned sage. But her fierce resolve to get the best of Seth leaped like wildfire a short time later. Tired of keeping the pace Seth and Copper set, she leaned forward in the saddle and urged Splotches into a full gallop over uneven ground, even though she knew better. "Can't that nag of yours keep up?" she shouted back to Seth.

The pound of hooves sang in Dori's ears, followed by Seth's, "Stop!" He pulled even with her and snatched the reins. Both horses came to a screeching halt.

Dori scorched with rage. "How dare you interfere."

"How dare you risk your horse by running her here?" Seth bellowed. Dori had never seen him so angry. "I didn't train Splotches just to have an idiot girl injure her by showing off. All it takes is one gopher hole to break a leg, not to mention what could happen to you."

Stung by feeling guilty and knowing that he was right, Dori still wouldn't give in. "As if you'd care. You're more concerned over Splotches getting hurt than you are about me. Fine teacher you are."

A curious expression crossed Seth's face. "If you get hurt, it's your own fault. Splotches has no say in whether she stays whole — and alive. Let's go home."

They rode in silence for a good mile before Dori blurted out, "Are you going to tell Matt?"

"That depends on you," Seth said with a look that boded no good for her. The twitch of a muscle in his cheek betrayed his wrath. "One more stunt like that, and I'm through. I agreed to ride herd on you to help Matt out, but if you're going to continue being a blasted nuisance, the deal is off."

Dori felt like she was bleeding inside from Seth's condemnation. Today's escapade had surely killed all hopes of her ever gaining Seth's respect — respect she suddenly realized she had craved from the time she returned to the Diamond S. Now all was lost because of her stubborn determination to have her own way.

FIFTEEN

Zing.

Dori's lasso sang through the air from her position atop her pinto mare. It captured the target stump for the fifth time in a row.

"Good job." Seth called from Copper's back. Ever since he'd read the riot act to her about racing Splotches, Dori had settled down and worked hard to master the tasks he gave her. Seth frowned. Working hard didn't hide the biding-my-time expression she sometimes still wore. Sure as the sun came up in the east, sooner or later Dori would rebel again.

Seth shook his head and watched Dori coil her lasso for another throw. He'd known taking charge of her would be tougher than chasing rustlers. What he hadn't counted on, but was forced to admit, was his growing admiration for the plucky girl.

You also didn't count on falling in love with her.

Seth set his jaw. Ha! That's just what he was *not* going to do. So what if his heart beat faster when she came running out to go riding? Or the softness in her manner at times indicated she might not be indifferent to him? No way would he consider anyone with her attitude as a possible life companion.

"You're my Trailmate, God," Seth mumbled for the dozenth time. "The woman I marry has to put You first in her life. Dori's aim in life seems to be having good times and her own way. Once she sets her mind, she's as immovable as El Capitan." Seth grinned. Miss Dolores Sterling would not appreciate being likened to the thirty-six-hundred-foot granite mass reaching for the sky in the Yosemite Valley, but the comparison was accurate.

Her voice interrupted Seth's soliloquy. "I'm tired of roping, Seth. Can we do something else? Practice jumping, maybe?"

"Only if you ride Copper. Splotches isn't trained enough yet to be safe jumping."

"Pooh." Dori patted her pinto's neck and looked rebellious. "Just because she balked and tossed me off doesn't mean she isn't ready. I simply wasn't prepared for her to stop." She grinned. "You didn't mean it, did you Splotches?"

143

The mare whinnied as if in agreement but it didn't change Seth's mind. "Either ride Copper, or no jumping," he ordered.

Dori's deep sigh sounded like it came from her boots. "Well, all right. Copper is a good horse, too."

Fighting words. *A good horse?* Are you blind? Copper's the best and most dependable horse on the Diamond S except for Matt's buckskin, Chase."

Dori bristled. Red flags waved in her cheeks. "He is not. I'll show you." She kicked Splotches with her boot heels and galloped away, straight for the narrow draw where she'd been thrown the day before.

"Stop." Seth leaped into Copper's saddle and took off after her.

"Never!" the flying figure called. "Faster, Splotches."

The mare responded with a burst of speed that sent chills through Seth. Had Dori regained enough of her riding skills to handle the mare? Seth shook out his coiled lariat. "Run, Copper." The sorrel sprang forward. Heart in his throat, Seth swung his lariat in a wide circle over his head.

Splotches reached the narrow gap in the earth and faltered just enough to break her stride. But when Dori called, "Go," the pinto sailed into the air and made it to the other side. She slid to a stop and Dori jumped from the saddle. "I told you she could do it."

Copper cleared the draw. Seth didn't miss a twirl of his lariat. The triumph in Dori's eyes triggered anger so strong that he flung the lasso. The rope fell over Dori and tightened before Seth realized what he was doing. It was as natural as roping a stubborn little calf but not nearly as pleasurable. Copper came to a standstill, and Seth slid from the saddle. Three long strides brought him face-to-face with the impossible girl.

Dori struggled against the lasso. "Let me go," she shouted, "or do you plan to hog-tie me on Splotches and take me back to the ranch?"

Seth saw fear in Dori's eyes in spite of her reckless words. Good. He had tried reasoning with her. It hadn't worked. Neither had threatening to stop the lessons and tell Matt why. Seth freed her, coiled his lariat, and hung it on the saddle horn. With one giant stride, he grabbed Dori by the shoulders, shook her until her hat sailed off, and said through gritted teeth, "For once in your life you're going to get what's coming to you, Dori Sterling."

"Let me go!" she screamed.

"Not until you've learned your lesson." Heedless of the consequences, Seth dropped to one knee, turned the struggling girl over the other, and whacked the back of her riding skirt — not hard enough to hurt her, but until dust flew.

"You — you . . ." Dori tore herself free and bounded to her feet. "I thought you were a Christian and a gentleman. You're no better than Red Fallon."

Seth's temporary insanity fled. He felt sick. What had he done? "I reckon you're right. I'll pack my gear and be off the ranch before night falls." He mounted Copper and looked down at her. "One thing, Miss Sterling. There's no excuse for my smacking you, but folks are treated the way they deserve to be treated. You may want to take a look at yourself before condemning me. Let's go, Copper." The sorrel leaped forward, leaving Dori alone with Splotches.

Dori watched until horse and rider were out of sight, then sank to the ground. She buried her face in her hands, feeling again the humiliation of being spanked like a naughty child. Yet Seth's words overshadowed all else.

"I'll pack my gear and be off the ranch before night falls. . . . Folks are treated the way they

146

deserve to be treated. You may want to take a look at yourself before condemning me."

"Dear God, what have I done? Worse, what is Matt going to say?"

The thought cut through Dori's misery and brought her to her feet. Matt must never know. It would break his heart to learn that the cowboy he loved and trusted had laid hands on Dori, even though she deserved it.

"I'm the only one who can make sure Matt doesn't find out," Dori muttered. She ran to Splotches, mounted, and prodded the mare into a gallop in the direction Seth had taken. Wind burned her face, but she didn't care. She must overtake Seth before he reached the Diamond S. It would be just like him to feel he must confess what had happened when he told Matt he was leaving — and his going would devastate Sarah.

What about you? the wind mocked.

Dori shook off the thought and bent low over Splotches' neck, urging her forward with every muscle in her body and praying that Seth wasn't too far ahead to be caught. She rounded a bend. Relief nearly unseated her. Copper stood beneath a huge oak tree just ahead. Seth leaned against the mighty trunk, head bowed and shoulders slumped.

Dori raced toward them and reined in the

pinto. Seth looked up. The suffering in his face went straight to Dori's heart. She slid to the ground. "Don't go." She reached out and clutched his hands.

Seth's mouth fell open. "You want me to stay? After what I did? Why?"

Not willing to confess what lay in her tumultuous heart, Dori stammered, "Because I . . . you . . . what difference does it make?" The shadow didn't leave his eyes so she added, "It was as much my fault as yours. I'm sorry."

Seth gripped her hands until they ached. "I'm the one who's sorry. I hope Matt will forgive me."

"He won't ever know," Dori flashed. "Didn't you tell me when you started 'riding herd' on me that it would be without interference from anyone? That works two ways."

The radiance in Seth's face when he freed her hands set a candle glowing in Dori's heart. It sparked an idea to convince Seth she was sincere. Could she do it? She must. Heart thundering, Dori gathered her nerve and said, "There's one condition."

A wary look crept back into Seth's eyes. "Which is . . . ?"

She took a deep breath. "Will you escort me to the barn raising?"

Dull red surged into Seth's tanned cheeks. "I can't."

Dori fell back. Embarrassment flowed through her like a river when Seth added, "Any man would be proud to escort you, but I've already invited Abby."

"I see. Have fun." Fighting tears of disappointment and anger at herself for making the preposterous suggestion, Dori climbed back on Splotches. "We'd best go home. It looks like rain."

"I'm sorry," Seth said, while swinging into Copper's saddle. "I had no idea you would ever consider going with me."

Pride forced Dori to raise her chin. "I wouldn't have if it had been any day but today." *Oh yeah?* her conscience jabbed. She turned Splotches, praying to make it home without betraying her further humiliation.

They rode silently until they reached one of the streams that fed the Fresno River. The stream was swollen and churning from recent rains. "Now what?" Dori asked.

Seth cast a glance toward the darkening sky, then up and down the stream. "We're a long way from home. If we go back the way we came, it will be pitch black before we get there. We should be all right crossing here. It's the only really good place for miles. Change horses with me."

Dori silently obeyed, and Seth adjusted both sets of stirrups.

"I'll go first. Come on, Splotches, show your stuff." Seth gave Dori a tight-lipped smile and nudged Splotches down the steep bank. Dori watched the pinto gingerly step forward, then begin to swim. Splotches appeared nervous, but Seth kept a firm hand on the reins. Dori could see he was talking to the horse, although the roar of the stream drowned out his words. They scrambled out of the water, up the opposite bank, and Seth beckoned to Dori.

"Our turn, Copper," Dori told the sorrel. He snorted and stepped into the flooded stream. All went well until they were halfway across. A floating tree, several branches still intact, barreled down the stream and blocked their way. Copper swerved to avoid the obstacle. The current caught him broadside. He staggered and regained his balance but had already been swept past the bank where Seth and Splotches waited.

Terror filled Dori, but she hung on for dear life. "You can do it, Copper," she encouraged, sticking in the saddle like a burr.

The sorrel tried again and again, but he could not out-swim the tree. Tossed by the current, it stayed between horse, rider, and the opposite bank. Dori didn't dare try to turn back. The bank was too steep to climb even if they could make it.

They rounded a sharp bend. A short distance ahead, another stream gushed white water into the one where she and Copper were trapped, changing it into a river. Unless they could get out before they reached that point, it meant certain death. Only God could save them now. "Please, God, help us," Dori cried.

Copper stumbled, bringing a fresh spurt of fear, but Dori whispered, "God, I know Your promises are sure. 'When thou passest through the waters, I will be with thee; and through the rivers, they shall not overflow thee.'" A mighty bellow from the opposite shore where Seth and Splotches were racing alongside the bank of the stream caught her attention.

"Let go of the reins. Raise your hands over your head. Take your feet out of the stirrups." Horse and rider plunged into the water.

Dori's throat dried. Following Seth's orders meant she could be swept out of the saddle.

"Trust me, Dori!"

She obeyed and swayed in the saddle.

Only the pressure of her thighs against Copper's heaving sides kept her upright.

The next instant a rope dropped over her raised arms and tightened. A mighty yank threw Dori out of the saddle and into the river. She desperately tried to keep her head up — and prayed for Seth. Just when she felt she couldn't make it, Seth and Splotches hauled her out of the flood. She lay on the bank, numb from cold and whispering, "Thank You, God."

Seth's voice roused her. "We have to find shelter." He sounded so grim it roused Dori from her misery. She sat up. Splotches stood with head down. Seth looked as if he'd lost his best friend.

Dori glanced back at the flooded stream — and understood. "Copper?"

Seth's expression and the slump of his shoulders cut into Dori's heart like sharp knives. She'd never heard such agony in anyone's voice than when Seth said, "He's gone."

Dori's tears gushed, but Seth helped her up.

"We have to get going. Can you walk? Splotches is tuckered out."

"Yes." It was all Dori could get out past the boulder-sized lump in her throat. She silently trudged after Seth and the pinto, away from the river that had taken Copper. Water sloshed in her boots. A keen wind cut through her clothing. She didn't complain. What was her discomfort compared with Seth's loss of the horse he loved?

What felt like a lifetime later, Seth led Splotches and Dori down a rocky ravine and stopped in front of a large clump of bushes. He parted them and grunted. "Good. We're on the right track."

Dori stared at the opening in the rock wall. Her hands went clammy, and she felt faint. Memories rushed over her: tall buildings in San Francisco and Boston threatening to squeeze the life out of her. The crowd of people in the Chicago train depot, pressing her in on all sides. Being trapped in the train car, knowing an avalanche could bury her alive.

Dori's fear and horror culminated in a wail. She put her hands over her face, backed away, and pleaded, "A cave? Please, Seth, don't make me go into a cave."

Sixteen

Pity for the shivering girl who stumbled away from the large hole in the rock wall filled Seth. Two agonized voices rang in his ears: Dori's plea, *"Please, Seth, don't make me go into a cave."* and Matt's concern when he learned his sister was trapped in the snowbound railway car: *"Confinement in small spaces terrifies Dori. It always has."*

Now her face shone pale as death in the growing dusk. Naked fear darkened her eyes until they looked midnight black. Seth ached for what he had to do but set his jaw and quietly said, "I'm sorry, Dori. We have no choice. This is the only shelter for miles around." His voice roughened, and pain flooded through him. "Copper's gone. Even if he were here, we couldn't get back to the ranch tonight. It's getting dark, and Splotches is in no condition to travel. Neither are we."

"Y–you d–don't understand," Dori spit

out between chattering teeth. "If my life d–depended on it, I c–couldn't g–go in the c–cave."

Seth steeled himself against her appeal. "You can, and you will." He hated the role he'd been forced to play but knew he must not weaken. "The cave is large enough for all three of us. I'll have a fire blazing in no time so we can dry our clothes." When Dori just stared at him, he took a deep breath and snapped, "I thought you were a thoroughbred, Miss Sterling. Stop acting like a baby and get in the cave. If you don't, I'll pack you in."

She was obviously too tired and cold to defy him. "Please, Seth. Don't make me go in there."

It was all Seth could do to resist her appeal, but in such dire circumstances, he dared not show it. "I will do whatever's necessary," he said. "Matt put me in charge of you on my terms. Now get in that cave, and get in there now."

For a moment, he thought she would refuse; then with a look that cut him to the heart, she stepped into the cave and hovered as close as she could to one side of the entrance. "I hate you for this, Seth Anderson."

"I know." Seth herded Splotches inside.

"Stand next to her until I get a fire going," he told Dori. "You can get some body heat from her."

Dori silently nudged the pinto between her and the dark rock wall at the back of the cave, keeping her own position as near the entrance as possible.

Seth quickly gathered dry oak leaves and pine needles blown into the floor of the cave. He stacked them into a tepee-shaped pile, then strode outside and brought in great armfuls of downed pine branches. Moments later, a roaring fire just inside the entrance banished the chill.

Dori needed no invitation to step close to the blaze. Steam rose from her sodden clothing, and she huddled in the welcome warmth, slowly turning as if on a spit. Seth rejoiced to see some of the fear leave her face and a bit of color return. Heedless of his own discomfort, he unsaddled Splotches and removed the saddle blanket, which had miraculously stayed fairly dry except near the edges.

"Hold one side," Seth told Dori. "As soon as it's dry, you have to get out of your wet clothes. Give yourself a good rubdown with the blanket, and wrap up in it. You can't stay in those wet clothes overnight." Seth held his breath, wondering what to do if she refused, which she probably would. He gave an audible sigh of relief when she nodded instead of arguing.

"Good girl. Things could be a lot worse. We're safe, and we'll soon be dry. But I'm afraid there'll be no supper. It's too dark to hunt, and fishing in that swollen creek is out of the question."

His remark earned him a small smile from Dori.

"I'm not very musical," Seth added. "My stepsister Ellianna is the one with a singing voice. But being here reminds me of an old hymn." He began singing:

"Rock of ages, cleft for me,
Let me hide myself in Thee;
Let the water and the blood,
From Thy wounded side which flowed,
Be of sin the double cure,
Save from wrath and make me pure."

For a long moment, Dori didn't respond. Then she said, "Thank you. We really are hiding in a rock, aren't we?" Her face gleamed in the firelight, and her fingers clenched and unclenched.

Seth's heart soared. Dori had opened the door for him to speak a word for his Master. "Yes, but Jesus, the Rock of ages, is truly our shelter. We never need be afraid, no matter how bad the storm." *Lord, let her know how true this is,* he silently prayed. To his disappointment Dori only said,

"I think the blanket is dry enough now. If you don't mind, I'll step into my dressing room and change." She took the warm blanket, squared her shoulders, and walked around behind Splotches.

Seth knew from the tilt of her head that leaving the bright fire for the darkness at the back of the cave was one of the hardest things Dori had ever done, but she didn't falter. When she said in a determined, but shaky voice, "Keep singing, will you?" he had never admired her more. He bellowed until the echoes rang from the rock ceiling and walls, "Rock of ages, cleft for me, / Let me hide myself in Thee."

He also prayed with all his might that the night would hold no further terrors for Dori; then he stripped branches from the pine limbs to make a bed for her near the fire.

Long after Dori lay asleep, wrapped in the saddle blanket like an Egyptian mummy, Seth kept watch. The firelight played on her exposed face. "So young and defenseless, in spite of all her bravado," he murmured. Had she really meant it when she said she hated him? After they reached the Diamond S, how would she feel? Would she remember God's goodness in helping Seth's lasso fly strong and true? Would she appreciate the dreaded cave where they had found shelter? Would she consider the things Seth had told her? Or would she only remember the humiliation he had seen in her face when she asked him to take her to the barn raising and he refused? And the way he had laid hands on her in a moment he would always regret?

Seth sighed. His head drooped. How could he have let the iron grip on his emotions loosen? Fear for Dori's safety when he saw Splotches leap the draw was no excuse. No matter what the provocation, he should have been able to control himself.

All through the long, dark hours, Seth kept the fire going and relived the day's events. Pain for losing Copper settled to a dull ache. No more would they fly over the range or stop to rest on the promontory that overlooked the valley. There would be other horses, but none would ever replace the sorrel gelding Seth's father had given him what seemed like a lifetime ago.

Just before dawn, fatigue replaced sadness and self-recrimination. Seth fell into an uneasy sleep. The nicker of a horse awakened him. His pulse quickened and he sat upright. "Copper?"

"No. It's only Splotches," a soft voice said. "I'm so sorry about Copper."

Seth's spurt of hope died. He rubbed sleep from his eyes and sprang to his feet. Dori, fully dressed and holding the saddle blanket, stood watching him. Sympathy shone in her blue eyes. Seth couldn't read her expression other than knowing it wasn't hatred. "Let's go home. I'm starved," she said.

In spite of his misery over losing Copper, Seth rejoiced. Except for tangled hair and a dirty face, Dori looked none the worse for her dunking in the creek. He couldn't say the same for himself. It seemed they had been away from the ranch for a week instead of less than a day. "All you can think of is your stomach," he teased. "What about the worry we've caused our folks?"

Dori's grin showed the unplanned night in the cave had dampened but not drowned her high spirits. "Why should they worry? They know you'll take care of me." Leaving Seth gasping, she demanded, "Well, are you coming? Or do I have to ride Splotches home and send someone back to get you?"

Lord, if I live to be older than the Sierras I

160

will never understand Dori Sterling, Seth silently confessed. *In less than a day, I've seen her change her mood more times than a day in March. One thing for certain: Whoever marries her will never be bored.*

Once outside the cave, Seth saddled the pinto. After the trio climbed out of the ravine, he made Dori ride while he walked beside her. He shuddered, thinking of the distance they had to cover before reaching the ranch. Even if Matt and the hands were out searching for them, Seth and Dori were far afield from where they had planned to ride. It would hamper the search party.

Shortly after the sun climbed over the top of a nearby hill, a shrill whistle split the morning air. Then another. A bunch of riders rode into sight, with Matt and Curly in front and Bud leading a saddled horse.

"How did they find us?" Dori cried.

"I don't know, but I'm mighty glad they did," Seth replied. He snatched off his Stetson and waved. *"Yippee-ki-ay!"*

Answering yells came back from the rescue party, and a few minutes later, they surrounded Seth and Dori. "Are you all right?" Matt asked.

"We're fine, especially now that you've come." Dori smiled. "We spent the night in a cave, and —"

"A cave?" Matt's jaw dropped, and he shot Seth a quick glance.

Dori's smile wobbled. "It was a very nice cave, as caves go, if you like that sort of thing." The next moment her eyes filled with tears. "If Seth hadn't been there yesterday I'd have died." Bright drops spilled from her eyes, and her face twisted. "Oh, Matt, the river took Copper."

Matt's mouth dropped open; then he reared back in the saddle and laughed. "Well, it may have taken him, but it gave him back. Copper was standing outside the corral this morning, wet and tired, but not hurt. That's how we found you — by following his tracks."

Could a man burst with happiness? Seth's, "Thank God!" mingled with Dori's delighted cry. Their gazes met. Locked. Dori's expression after all the hours of worry and fear made Seth's eyes sting. His joy at knowing Copper was safe and waiting reflected in the girl's eyes like twin bonfires. No matter what might come, he would carry that look in his heart and cherish it.

Seth's joy continued until they reached the ranch. The stable hands had already cared for Copper, but Seth patted his horse and whispered to him before cleaning up and heading to Solita's kitchen for a much-needed meal. His good mood, however, died when Katie O'Riley joined them for a cup of coffee and brought up the last subject Seth wanted discussed.

"Miss Dori, what's a barn raising?" she innocently asked. "Curly asked if I'd go with him, but I don't for the life of me know what 'tis." She shook her curly red head and chuckled. "How can a barn get raised up? For sure not like Lazarus in the Bible."

Seth avoided looking at Dori but couldn't ignore the ice in her voice when she said, "When a neighbor's barn burns or falls down, folks for miles around gather early in the morning to raise — build — a new one. The womenfolk bring food enough to feed a regiment, and there's a square dance at the end of the day when the building is done."

Seth couldn't help stealing a look at Dori. His heart sank and he lost his appetite. The tilt of her pretty chin boded no good for one Seth Anderson.

"Curly will be a wonderful escort and you will have a lot of fun, Katie." She paused and sent Seth a disdainful glance. "So will Seth. He's taking Abby, you know."

"The pretty young lady who works at the Yosemite Hotel?" Katie's green eyes

163

sparkled. "She's a fine colleen, I'm for think-ing."

Dori shoved back from the table. "She is. Any man would be proud to take her." She left the room with her head high.

Katie looked stricken. "Did I say some-thing wrong?"

Seth forced a smile and stood, leaving half his breakfast uneaten. "No, Katie. Miss Do-lores is just tired." But he winced as he went out. Dori had parroted the very words he'd used when turning down her invitation to the barn raising. Seth sighed. Hang it all, he'd only invited Abby because she'd taken for granted that he'd escort her. This was what came of paying attention to only one girl at a time. Would Dori ever forgive him for refusing the invitation it had obviously cost her dearly to make — an invitation Seth suspected would never be repeated?

SEVENTEEN

Dori slowly trudged up the staircase on feet that felt heavier than lead. Exhaustion and disappointment washed through her like the waves of the swollen stream that had threatened to overwhelm her.

"Don't be a ninny," she ordered herself. "You should be glad Curly invited Katie to the barn raising. You don't want him, so why feel betrayed? Curly, Bud, Slim, and a dozen others have practically camped on your doorstep ever since you came home. You've laughed at them. It's natural for them to be attracted to Katie."

Katie? a little voice mocked. *This has nothing to do with her or with the cowboys. You're jealous of Abby Sheridan because Seth Anderson is paying attention to her and taking her to the barn dance.*

"That's stupid!" Dori exclaimed as she burst through her bedroom doorway.

Solita looked up from turning down the

covers on Dori's bed. Her round, brown face showed surprise at Dori's outburst. "What is stupid, querida?"

Solita was not the person Dori wanted to face right then. The housekeeper's dark, knowing gaze saw far too much. Keeping secrets from Solita was like trying to keep the sun from rising.

"I'm just mumbling," Dori quickly said, then blurted out the last thing she wanted to discuss. "Did you know that Curly invited Katie to the barn raising?"

Solita's wide, white smile deepened the laugh crinkles around her eyes. "Sí. Señor Curly admires our Señorita Katie. She returns his regard."

The news jolted Dori. "She does? How do you know?"

"Is your head so far up in the clouds that you cannot see what is happening under your very nose? Unless my eyes deceive me, Señorita Katie will be Señora Prescott *muy pronto.*" Solita plumped the pillows and patted Dori on the shoulder. "Now you must rest." She smiled and went out, closing the door behind her.

Dori doubted she could stay awake long enough to don night clothes and tumble into her soft, welcoming bed. "It sure is different from the pine branches in the cave," she muttered. The thought roused her from the stupor into which her tired body was sinking. A multitude of memories pounded her weary brain. Scene after scene replayed, clarified by hindsight and accusing her in no uncertain terms. "If I hadn't defied Seth by jumping Splotches over the draw, I wouldn't have been humiliated, almost drowned, and forced to spend the night in a cave," she whispered.

An all-too-familiar rush of fear made her tremble, followed by the memory of Seth's voice when he said, *"Jesus, the Rock of ages, is truly our shelter. We never need be afraid, no matter how bad the storm."*

The words stilled the tumult in Dori's soul like no amount of reasoning or berating herself had ever been able to do. She remembered how safe she'd felt, wrapped in the saddle blanket and knowing nothing could harm her while Seth kept watch. How vulnerable he had looked when she awakened to find him sleeping. Dark shadows beneath his eyes attested to the strain he had been through while hauling her out of the raging stream. The shadow of a beard as red-gold as Seth's hair showed on his usually clean-shaven face. Dori's first impression slipped into her mind: *everything Matt had said and more.*

Now a lump rose to her throat. Why did life have to be so hard? Why couldn't Seth love her, instead of Abby?

Dori cried herself to sleep.

The day of the barn raising came all too soon for Dori. Much to Bud and Slim's delight, she had accepted their gallant invitation to "es-cort" her, but she dreaded the event. Even the new, yellow-sprigged gown that made her hair look darker and her eyes bluer, failed to comfort her. "Lord, I'm going to need Your help," Dori impetuously prayed. "I can't beg off going. Even if I fooled everyone else, Solita would know why." She made a face at herself in the mirror and raised her chin. "If You'll help me make it through the day, I'll —"

"Come on, Dori, time's a-wasting," Matt sang out from the bottom of the staircase before Dori figured out what to promise God in return for His help. She wrapped herself in a cape against the early morning chill and lightly ran downstairs. Too bad she couldn't trip and twist an ankle.

Busy with women's work at the barn raising, Dori longed to be out riding Splotches. "Will this day never end?" she muttered to herself. Barn raising was a hard, hungry job and required a multitude of meals. Dori helped serve the horde of workers mid-morning sandwiches, cake, and lemonade; a hearty dinner; more sandwiches, cake, and lemonade in the midafternoon; and a full supper. In between, she listened to Sarah, Abby, Katie, and a bevy of other women and girls chatter, and assisted in washing a mountain of dishes. When she had a few moments to rest, she stepped outside and watched the barn going up under the magic of many willing hands.

By the time the kitchen chores ended and Dori threw out the final pan of dishwater, she never wanted to attend another barn raising. How could Katie, in her favorite green-checked gown, and Abby, radiant in pink, be so excited about the barn dance to follow? All Dori wanted to do was to crawl in a hole and pull it in after her.

She sighed. "Sterlings don't quit," she admonished herself. "Now get out there and be the belle of the ball." She grinned in spite of herself.

The first discordant notes of fiddles tuning up jangled in her ears. The three musicians swung into a lively hoedown. "Grab your partners, ladies and gents," the caller commanded. "Line up for the Virginia reel."

Bud reached Dori a few steps ahead of

Slim and led her to the head of the line. Matt grabbed Sarah. Curly and Katie came next, then Seth and Abby. A dozen other laughing couples took their places, men in a long line with their partners facing them.

"Swing your partner.

"Do-si-do.

"Allemande left.

"Grand right and left."

Dori's feet responded to the calls. Her reluctance gave way to enjoyment. When she encountered Seth and he swung her in time to the music and asked if she were having fun, she could honestly answer, "Yes."

"Feel like riding tomorrow?" he wanted to know.

"Of course." Dori's heart sang. Seth might be Abby's "*es*-cort," but the look in his eyes gave rise to a faint hope. The lively young woman had obviously set her cap for Seth, but he didn't appear to be roped and hogtied yet.

March gave way to April, April to May, then early June and time to drive the cattle to the high country, turn them loose, and let them graze until the fall roundup. Dori was wild to go. "Sarah's never seen the high country," she pleaded when Matt, Seth, and Solita violently opposed their going along.

"It's been years since I've been there. You won't mind roughing it for a couple of weeks, will you Sarah?"

Sarah's eyes glistened, but she sighed and said, "No, but if Matt thinks we shouldn't go, it's all right with me."

"It's not all right with *me.*" Dori crossed her arms and glared at her brother. "Brett says we'll be just fine and no trouble at all. Curly, Bud, and Slim can look after us."

"And who will be looking after the cattle?" Matt inquired in a deceptively mild tone.

"All of us." Dori smirked. "Sarah is a good rider. Seth says I have the makings of a great cowhand. I can ride and rope and shoot. Please, Matt, take us." She clasped her hands around his arm and met his gaze straight on.

Matt raised his hands in defeat. "Ganging up on me, are you?" He appealed to Katie, who sat nearby. "I suppose you want to go, too?"

"Me?" She gasped, eyes enormous. "Mercy, I never thought I'd be for doing such a thing. May I?"

Mischief glinted in Matt's eyes. "Why not? I won't have to tell Curly to look after you. Seems he's taken over that job on his own."

Katie turned red as a poppy. "Begging your pardon, sir, but you're for being a bit

171

of a spalpeen." She rose and shook out her skirts.

"And what might that be?"

"An Irish rascal, as you well know." She fled in the burst of laughter at Matt's expense. He turned to Solita.

"How about you?"

The housekeeper stared at him as if he had gone loco. "No, Señor Mateo. I will stay here and run the ranch while you are away."

Matt grunted. "Probably do a better job than Brett or me." He stood and stretched. "All right. We'll leave as soon as we can get ready."

Dori could hardly wait. She pestered Solita, who was in charge of making lists to ensure enough provisions were purchased, until the housekeeper staged a Mexican mutiny. "Out of my kitchen or there will be no trip."

Dori hugged her. "Sorry. It's just that I'm so excited. I love the high country."

Solita rolled her eyes. "I know." She chuckled. "Does it also have something to do with the fact a certain Señor Anderson is going?"

"Whatever do you mean?" Dori challenged. Not willing to hear the answer, she spun out of the kitchen and up to her room in order to hide her hot cheeks. "Not that it does any good." She sighed. "Solita has eyes like an eagle. She doesn't miss a thing."

It didn't take eagle eyes for Dori to see the stranger who descended on the Diamond S one afternoon a few days before the time set for departure to the high country. She was pulling on her boots by her open window and watching the activity at the corral. Curly, Bud, and Slim sat perched on the top fence of the corral observing Seth break a colt and jeering good-naturedly. A rig from the Madera livery pulled up.

Dori leaned forward. A stranger climbed out. The driver set two valises on the ground, nodded to the trio on the fence, and headed back for town.

Who on earth . . . ?

Dori felt hot blood flood her face. She blinked and looked at the stranger again. Her hand flew to her mouth to stifle a cry. No one on earth could be stranger than the person standing in her yard. The scarecrow-like man was clothed in someone's cockeyed idea of western apparel: A purple-and-white-striped satin shirt. Kelly green pants. Fringed chaps. Spanking new high-heeled boots — and the widest Stetson ever seen in California. Twin pistols in a low-slung holster belt completed Stancel Worthington

III's outfit. A mail-order cowboy, if Dori had ever seen one.

After a moment's hesitation, Stancel approached the fence and the staring cowboys, who were obviously struck dumb by the apparition. "I say. Where might I find Dolores Sterling?"

Curly, always the trio's spokesman, was evidently the first to recover his wits. "Miss Sterling may be out riding."

Dori suspected Curly bit his tongue to keep from adding, "Not that it's any of your business" and blessed him for his evasion. Curly knew perfectly well where she was — he'd waved to her just a few minutes earlier.

The answer obviously didn't faze "dear Stancel."

"I am Stancel Worthington III, of England and Boston," he announced in a haughty voice that made Dori long for one of her cowboys to flatten him. "I'm taking advantage of the summer break at the Brookside Finishing School for Young Ladies in Boston. I have come to tame Dolores, marry her, and take her back to civilization."

He produced a handkerchief and delicately held it to his nose. "My good man, please be so kind as to show me to my accommodations — as far away from this dreadful odor as possible."

174

Eighteen

The colt Seth had been breaking gave a final snort of independence, ended his fight against the inevitable, and stood quivering in the corral.

"Good boy." Seth patted the horse's neck, slapped him on the rump, and sent him flying. An explosion of mirth whipped Seth around. Curly, Bud, and Slim were draped over the fence howling and holding their sides. A stranger stood outside the fence glowering at the trio. Seth's jaw dropped in disbelief. The colors of the man's clothing far outshone even the outfits the guitar-strumming vaqueros wore on fiesta days.

Seth gave a low whistle.

Bud recovered enough to gasp, "The things a feller sees when he don't have a gun."

Seth joined in the laughter that followed. "Who's the tinhorn?" he inquired, his gaze never leaving the man outside the fence.

Curly sprang down from his perch, wiped tears of mirth from his eyes, and donned his most innocent expression. "Show some respect, Brother Anderson. This here gent says he's come all the way from England and Boston to marry up with Miss Dori. 'Course he has to tame her first, like she was a colt. Then he aims to take her back to civ'li-za-shun."

"His moniker's Stan-sell Worthington," Bud helpfully put in.

"The Third," Slim solemnly added. "Don't fergit the Third. Hey, Seth, d'yu s'pose the First and Second will be moseyin' along soon?"

The devilry in the cowboys' eyes and their outrageous drawls were contagious. Ever ready for fun, Seth decided to join in the byplay. He knew all about the arrogant Mr. Stancel Worthington III, who had caused Dori to get expelled from the fancy Boston school. Seth's blood boiled just thinking about it, even though it had brought her home where she belonged.

"If Dori's going to marry this long-nosed Englishman, I'm a ring-tailed raccoon," he muttered. A lightning glance toward the hacienda showed Dori watching through the open window of her upstairs room. Seth's heart leaped. What an opportunity to get even with Worthington on her behalf.

Seth grabbed the top fence rail, vaulted over it, and landed with a resounding *thud*. He wiped sweaty fingers on his vest and shook his hair down over his forehead. He stretched his mouth into a wide grin and crossed his eyes. Reaching Worthington in one long stride, he grabbed the visitor's hand.

"Welcome to this yere Diamond S," Seth said in a nasal twang that set the cowboys off into another paroxysm. He yanked Stancel's flaccid hand up and down as if priming a stubborn pump. "You done got yere just in time. I shore need help breakin' this colt. These lazy, no-count hands" — he sent a warning glance at the three compadres — "ain't worth a plugged nickel when it comes to breakin' horses." Seth tightened his grip. "Say, Mr. Third, how about *you* givin' it a go? I done got most of the ginger out of the ornery beast."

Stancel jerked his hand free. "My name is *Mr. Worthington.*" Icicles dripped from his words.

"Sorry." Seth dug the toe of his boot in the dust as if abashed, then looked up and confided, "You gotta make 'lowances fer Slim. He's done been tossed off broncs and lit on his noggin so much he ain't alwuz

177

quite right. Shall I round up the colt fer you?"

The ridiculously garbed man's pale gaze impaled him like a tomahawk in the hands of an expert. If looks could kill, Seth Anderson would be dead and buried on the spot. "I didn't travel thousands of miles into this godforsaken country to break horses or converse with a bunch of ruffians. I insist that you take me to my accommodations." His voice was muffled by the handkerchief he still held to his nose.

He spun on one high-heeled boot, tripped on an uneven spot in the ground, and sprawled full length just outside the dusty corral. Obviously stunned, he lay there blinking — until Dori Sterling exploded through the ranch house door. Her clear voice rang in the air.

"Just what are you doing on the Diamond S, *Mr. Worthington*?"

Seth's lips twitched. He started forward to help the man up, but Stancel rudely shoved Seth's extended hand aside in an obvious attempt to gather the remnants of his dignity. "You know why I came," he told Dori in a condescending voice. It stilled the laughter and brought Bud and Slim off the fence to align themselves next to Seth and Curly. "A Worthington always gets what he wants." Stancel cast a disparaging glance at the four cowboys, then back at Dori. "You should thank whatever gods there may be that I've come to save you from marrying one of these louts."

Dori's magnificent eyes shot blue sparks. "I'd marry any of my cowboys before I'd marry you," she blazed. "Where are those English manners you boast of having? Not one of these gentlemen would arrive on a girl's doorstep and tell a group of complete strangers he has come to marry her." She paused and took a deep breath.

"Yippee-ki-ay," Curly chortled, but Dori wasn't through.

"Western hospitality demands that we allow you to stay for a time, but I'm warning you: Watch your step. I don't know anything about how girls and young women in England are treated, but out here, folks hold them in high regard. Westerners get riled up real easy by anyone who persists in making a nuisance of himself." She flounced away, then sent a conspiratorial look back at Seth. "Show our visitor to the bunkhouse, will you, Seth? He can eat at the house, but I'm hoping the boys will teach him some things he needs to know."

"Yes, Miss Sterling." Seth picked up Worthington's valises and smothered a grin. As soon as he could get Curly, Bud, and Slim to one side, he'd put a bug in their ears and ask them to enlist the rest of the hands in a campaign guaranteed to send Stancel Worthington III packing. Aided and abetted by Dori, who had wordlessly made it clear she was throwing Stancel to the wolves, the boys would topple Stancel from his high horse in short order.

Dori had always laughed when Solita reminded her that Dolores meant "sorrows" or "sorrowful." But the day Stancel Worthington III arrived on the Diamond S was the beginning of misery. The insufferable man dogged her steps, either blind to Dori's contempt or convinced he could show her how far superior he was to any westerner. He seemed bent on impressing the "laughing hyenas" who jeered at him from the corral fence and in the bunkhouse. Ignoring advice about riding alone, the day following his arrival, Stancel took off by himself. An hour later, he dashed into the yard and up to the porch where the womenfolk were sitting with Matt and Seth.

"Rustlers. Out there." Stancel waved back over his shoulder.

"How do you know they were rustlers and not our hands?" Dori demanded.

"My dear woman, uncouth as they are, surely your employees wouldn't shoot at me." Stancel triumphantly exhibited a hole in his oversize hat.

Galvanized into action, a dozen men, including Matt and Seth, galloped off in pursuit of the cattle thieves, leaving Dori to stew over being left behind when she itched to be part of the chase. "It isn't fair," she blurted out. "I can ride and rope and shoot, and I own half the cattle."

Stancel looked horrified. "No lady hunts outlaws."

Dori rounded on him. "Will you get it through your thick head that I am not a lady? I never have been and never will be. Why don't you go back to Boston and marry Gretchen van Dyke?"

Stancel gave her what was as close to a leer as Dori could ever imagine him showing. "I . . . ah . . . Miss van Dyke does not possess one of the qualities I admire in you."

His remark stunned Dori, but she said in an imitation of Gretchen's simper, "And which quality, pray tell, is that?"

Stancel checked both ways, as if to make sure he wouldn't be overheard. His long face reddened. "A bit of fire. A man wants more than a pretty face."

Dori fled — and stayed in her room until

she heard the pound of hooves in the yard hours later. She rushed downstairs and outside, ignoring Stancel, who rose from a chair on the porch. Fear in her heart, she counted the riders. *Six. Seven. Eight. Nine.* Terror gripped her throat until she could barely breathe. "Where are the others?" she finally asked Matt. "Curly and Bud and" — her voice broke — "and Seth?"

Matt leaped down from his horse and caught her when she swayed. "They'll be along soon. Right now they're busy taking a couple of two-bit rustlers to Sheriff Meade and the Madera jail." He snorted. "The rustlers didn't put up much of a fight." Matt's forehead puckered. "I thought one might be Red Fallon. No such luck. In spite of rumors, it appears he's long gone from the valley. Good riddance." Matt went up the steps and plumped Dori into a chair.

"Thank God our hands are safe," Dori whispered.

Just then an unwelcome voice grated on her nerves. "I say, I'm a bit of a hero, right-o?" Stancel beamed at the assembled crowd.

"You? A hero?" The men's faces reflected Dori's incredulous exclamation.

Stancel puffed up until he looked like an overstuffed owl. "It's jolly well true. If I hadn't risked life and limb and been shot at, you wouldn't have known about the blighters, much less been able to catch them."

It was the last straw. For the second time that day, Dori fled, only this time it was amid shouts of glee that rang to the heavens at Stancel's taking credit for the arrest. Sick of the houseguest who showed every sign of staying until, as Matt put it, "The last dog is hung," Dori hatched a devious plan. A discussion at supper solidified it. As usual, Stancel took center stage. After Matt asked the blessing, Stancel said, "A family custom?" He helped himself generously to roast beef so tender it cut like butter and mounded mashed potatoes on his plate.

Dori opened her mouth to reply, but Matt beat her to it.

"In this house we give thanks to God for what He provides."

"How quaint. Commendable, of course, if one believes there is a God." Stancel stroked his chin with a bony finger. "I personally find it hard to swallow."

Matt laid down his fork and said, "God not only exists, He created and rules the world and all that is in it. He loved us so much that He sent His Son, Jesus Christ, to die on the cross so all who believe on Him might have eternal life. You appear to be a learned man, Mr. Worthington. Surely you have read John 3:16 in the Bible."

Stancel gave a dismissive wave. "Oh yes. Something Jesus Christ supposedly said. If Jesus really lived, He appears to have been a pretty good chap. Perhaps even a great teacher, but the Son of God? Surely you don't believe that."

Matt's voice rang. "I do. We all do. You are sadly mistaken. Jesus was not just a good man or a great teacher. He was either insane to claim divinity, the greatest liar who ever lived, or who He said He was — the Son of God. The subject is closed. There will be no more such talk in this house."

Stancel blinked and subsided, but Dori inwardly raged. Stancel had shown his true colors and removed any second thoughts she had about carrying out her brilliant plan.

NINETEEN

When Stancel spouted off about God at the supper table, Seth longed to shake the Englishman until he rattled. A quick look at Dori showed that for once they agreed. It also showed she was up to no good. Mutiny darkened her eyes and warned she'd hatched a plan designed to penetrate even Worthington's thick hide. Seth silently cheered. Stancel the Third needed straightening out.

Dori's voice yanked Seth from his musings. "I have something in mind that may interest you, Mr. Worthington. Do stay for a while after supper."

Seth noticed she avoided looking at the others around the table. No wonder. The sudden change from her frigid treatment of their self-invited guest to warm and friendly had caught even Seth off guard. Dori's barely concealed excitement verified his suspicions. He'd bet his bottom dollar it had to do with the upcoming cattle drive. Seth inwardly groaned. Stancel's purple and white satin shirt and fancy green pants were enough to stampede the herd.

When supper was over and everyone gathered in front of the sitting room fireplace, Dori fired her opening gun. Seth noted she directed her remarks to their guest.

"In a few days, we're going to drive a great many of our cattle to the high country," she said. Anticipation sparkled in her eyes. "Can you imagine the joy of sleeping out under the stars, breathing mountain air, and eating food prepared in a chuck wagon, Mr. Worthington?"

Seth grinned. Dori had scrupulously omitted mention of dust, ornery cows, possible storms, rattlesnakes, and the like. He stifled a laugh when she tossed out what was undoubtedly the clincher.

"Sarah and Katie and I are all going, but if you think it's too much for you, we'll understand. You're welcome to remain at the ranch."

The animation in Stancel's face told Seth all the wild horses in California wouldn't keep Worthington from the high-country trip.

He confirmed this by saying with more

spirit than Seth had seen him show, except after he'd been shot at by rustlers, "How ripping. When do we go?"

The conversation turned to planning but Seth scarcely heard it. For better or for worse, Stancel Worthington III would be on the cattle drive. And if Dori carried out whatever outrageous plan she obviously had in mind, it would be for the worse.

That night, Dori lay in bed, looking out her window at the stars. Her conscience jabbed. How fair was it to expose a greenhorn to the hardships of the trail?

"With so many real men along, nothing much can go wrong, God," she whispered. "The trip might even change Stancel's life. He made it plain at supper that he doesn't know You or Your Son. How can he not respond to the wonders of Your creation: the elk and pronghorn antelope, the rushing streams and pine-scented air? If they don't convince him there is Someone behind it all, Stancel will surely be affected by the deep faith Matt, Sarah, Seth, and even Katie display in everyday life."

She squirmed and sighed. "I have to admit, Lord, it won't be from watching me. I'm not much of a witness for You."

"You could be."

But Dori was too involved thinking of what tomorrow might bring to heed the quietly spoken message to her heart.

In spite of Stancel buzzing around Dori like a persistent mosquito, plus annoying the outfit with ridiculous suggestions, the cattle drive went well. Perfect weather prevailed, with mornings as crisp as Cookie's bacon and stentorian call, "Come an' git it before I throw it out." Sunny afternoons and glorious star-studded nights followed.

"I'm more alive than I ever was in Boston," Dori told Seth the afternoon they reached the high country and turned the cattle loose. "I haven't forgiven Miss Brookings, but I'm so glad to be home that her accusations don't bother me as much." Dori's laughter trilled. "Still, revenge is sweet. If only Genevieve could see 'dear Stancel' now." She pointed to the disheveled man, unkempt from life on the trail. "She would clasp her hands in horror and pray for her nephew to be delivered from the savage West . . . and from me."

"He sure is a sorry sight," Seth observed.

Dori smirked. "You ain't seen nothin' yet."

Suspicion flickered in Seth's eyes. "What's that supposed to mean?"

"Wait and see."

188

That night around the campfire Matt announced, "We'll head back to the Diamond S tomorrow."

In spite of Stancel's presence, Dori didn't want the trip to end. "Matt, can we go home by way of the logging camp? I haven't been there since I was a little girl, but I remember how lumber from the sawmill boomed down that sixty-mile flume to Madera." She added, "It's sure to interest Sarah and Katie and Mr. Worthington. Seth, too, if he hasn't been there."

"I've seen it," Seth agreed. "It's a sight to behold."

"Wouldn't you like to see it, Stancel?" Dori held her breath waiting for his answer.

Obviously saddlesore and weary of the woods, Stancel hesitated, then said, "Perhaps I should, since this is my only chance. Once we're married and living in Boston we won't return to California."

Any chance of Dori abandoning her latest and most diabolical plan vanished. She felt hot and cold by turns but finally broke the stunned silence. "It is your only chance to see the flume, Mr. Worthington."

A murmur rippled through the circle around the fire, but Matt quickly said, "I doubt the hands want to visit a lumber camp. They'll want to get back to the ranch."

A chorus of approval confirmed Matt's statement, but Curly looked at Katie and drawled, "I don't mind stayin'. Without the bawlin' critters, we can make good time on the way home. Say, Boss, why don't you send Cookie and the chuck wagon back? I'm a pretty fair camp cook. Besides, Mr. Worthington can help me."

Dori's hand flew to her mouth. Leave it to Curly to come up with such an idea.

Stancel only tucked his chin into his neck and declined. "I'm afraid I wouldn't be much good at such demeaning chores."

Curly put his hands on his hips and glared, but Katie piped up.

"I've never cooked out in the open, Curly, but if you'll be for teaching me, I'll be glad to help." Her offer raised an outcry from the cowboys.

"Aw, Boss, if I'd know Miss Katie was gonna be assistant cook an' bottle washer, I'da volunteered to stay," Bud protested.

"Me, too," Slim growled.

Curly smirked. "Too late, pards. See you back at the ranch."

His disgruntled friends marched off, leaving Dori filled with glee.

It didn't last. The departure of the outfit

190

left her vulnerable to Stancel's unwelcome wooing. When not busy with the cattle, Curly, Bud, and Slim had foiled the easterner's attempts to get Dori away from the crowd. Now it took all Dori's cunning to avoid being alone with him. Matt and Sarah were still in the honeymoon stage and often wandered off together. Curly appeared unwilling to let Katie out of his sight. That left Seth to protect Dori. Instead, he infuriated her by standing aside and acting amused at her predicament.

One afternoon, Stancel followed Dori to a shady glade where she'd gone to hide from him. Taking her by surprise, he pinned her arms and attempted to kiss her. Dori jerked free and slapped his face with a resounding *crack*. Tears of rage stung her eyes.

Stancel shrugged. "Why fight the inevitable? Remember, Worthingtons always get what they want."

Dori raced back to camp, vowing to show him up so badly he'd tuck his tail between his legs and slink back to Boston.

A full moon and a crackling campfire on the night the travelers reached Sugar Pine Logging Camp and the flume gave Dori the perfect opportunity. She encouraged Matt to relate some of the local legends. She then added, "Of all the escapades concerning the

Sierra Nevada area, the most thrilling is 'riding the flume.' Daring men jump into crude, sixteen-foot boats called 'hog troughs' or 'hog boats.' They are lowered into the gushing water as it cascades from the mountains down to the valley."

"Yes, and it's both dangerous and fool-hardy," Matt snapped.

Dori didn't give an inch. "I admire anyone brave enough to ride the flume." The grow-ing interest in Stancel's face showed how well her scheme was working. "I'd ride a hog boat myself except that Matt would skin me alive."

"You've got that right, little sister. Remem-ber what happened to H. J. Ramsdell?" Matt didn't wait for her answer. "The *New York Tribune* reporter, two millionaires, and a drunken carpenter rode a flume back in 1875. Ramsdell climbed to the top of the trestlework to see the huge logs roar down the flume. He later wrote, 'It was like the rushing of a herd of buffalo.' "

"What happened?" a wide-eyed Sarah asked.

Dori said nothing. She'd heard the story since childhood. Now she secretly gloated. Stancel's enthralled attention showed that tomorrow would repay everything she'd suf-fered at his hands.

"The two-hundred-pound Ramsdell thought if the millionaires could afford to risk their lives, so could he. Only one of the fifty mill hands and loggers standing around agreed to go with them. An experienced flume shooter warned, 'You can't stop, or lessen your speed. Sit still, shut your eyes, say your prayers, take all the water that comes . . . and wait for eternity.'

"The hog trough was lowered into the flume. The carpenter jumped into the front and Ramsdell into the stern, with a millionaire in the middle. The second millionaire leaped into a boat behind them. When the terrified reporter finally opened his eyes, they were streaking down the mountainside. The trestle was seventy feet high in some places. Lying down, Ramsdell could see only the flume stretching for miles ahead. He thought he would suffocate from the wind. The hog trough hit an obstruction. The drunk carpenter was thrown into the flume and had to be dragged back inside.

"The second boat crashed into the first. Another man was hurled into the water. Splintered boats and bodies slid the rest of the way to the bottom of the flume."

"I say, old chap, it sounds like jolly good fun," Stancel exclaimed, eyes gleaming.

"Are you a raving lunatic? Those men fell fifteen miles in thirty-five minutes. They were more dead than alive when they reached a place where they could get off." He stood. "Enough of such stories, folks. Time to hit the sack. Tomorrow comes early."

Dori stayed to stare into the fire after the others left, then started to get up. A firm grip on her shoulder pressed her back down. *How dare Stancel touch me.* She whirled and froze. "You."

"Yes, me," Seth spit out. "I'd like to wring your pretty neck. Pranks like putting a wet rope under Worthington's tarp and making him think it was a snake is one thing. Goading someone into a situation where he can be injured or killed is a different story. Wasn't slapping Stancel when he tried to kiss you enough punishment?"

Dori scrambled to her feet. Embarrassment surged through her. "You saw?"

"I did." Seth crossed his arms and his face looked like a thundercloud in the dim light. "I despise Worthington's attitude, but he's still a human being, created in the image of the God he doesn't believe exists. What if Stancel dies while showing off for you, trying to prove he can do everything westerners do? Is 'getting even' worth knowing someone may be hurled into eternity without God?"

Dori saw in Seth's clear eyes what her conscience had been trying to tell her. Sickness rose from the pit of her stomach. Sickness and the knowledge she had demeaned herself in Seth's eyes. How could she have allowed the desire for revenge to carry her to such unspeakable lengths? She grabbed Seth's arm, fear washing away everything but the need to undo what she had wrought. "You don't think Stancel really means to ride the flume, do you?"

"I believe he will do anything to impress you."

Horrified, Dori cried, "We have to stop him."

Seth's strong hand covered hers, but he sounded defeated. "I only hope we can."

TWENTY

"I only hope we can."

The concern in Seth's voice about Stancel riding the flume haunted Dori and robbed her of sleep. What if they couldn't stop him? Dori took a long, quivering breath. What had she done? She knew from past experience that once Stancel set his mind, his stubbornness made the most uncooperative mule on the ranch look tractable as a lamb.

Dori planned to approach Stancel first thing in the morning, but she couldn't get him alone. Sugar Pine Camp buzzed with activity, and for the first time since Stancel arrived at the ranch, he appeared to be avoiding her.

"If I say anything in front of the others, he will ride the flume just to save face," Dori reasoned. "He didn't actually say he was going to do it. Surely when he sees the hog troughs, he will back down."

That's what you think, her conscience

jeered. *What if Matt has to tell Miss Brookings her nephew drowned while trying to show he has more courage than the experienced loggers and mill hands who are smart enough not to jeopardize their lives?*

The thought sickened Dori but steeled her determination. She must stop Stancel at all costs, even if it meant groveling. She hated doing so but had no choice. If that didn't work, she would ask Matt to start them back to the ranch immediately. Muleheaded as Stancel was, he wouldn't defy his host.

Dori caught up with Stancel at the top of the flume a few minutes before the rest of the Diamond S party arrived. He stood with a group of loggers who were obviously dumbstruck with his garish outfit. Gaze fixed on a hog boat tied at the head of the flume, Stancel's expression made Dori's flesh creep. She forced a laugh through a throat dried with fear.

"It's quite a sight, isn't it?" She pitched her voice so only he could hear and pointed to the rushing water encased in a V-shaped trough that zigzagged down the hillside "You can see why it takes a fool to attempt riding the flume. I apologize for what I said last night. I don't really admire men who do stupid things. I was just spouting off."

"Reah-ly." Stancel turned from staring at

197

the flume and looked down his long nose at her. "Nevertheless, I intend to go. It will be the thrill of a lifetime."

Dori froze. "Your lifetime may be mighty short if you insist on riding the flume."

He ignored her.

She raced back to her brother who, along with the rest of the party, had caught up with them. "Stancel is determined to ride the flume," she cried. "Stop him, Matt."

Matt leaped from Chase's back and strode toward the Englishman. "Get this and get it straight, Worthington. No one in his right mind, especially a foolhardy easterner, is going to ride the flume while I'm around."

A rumble of agreement rose from the loggers.

"Rubbish. You have no right to tell me what I can and cannot do."

Cold chills rushed up and down Dori's spine at the sneer in Stancel's voice.

Matt's eyes flashed in the way that warned of trouble ahead for anyone who crossed him. "*You are not riding the flume.* Seth, Curly, bring your lassoes. We'll hog-tie this fool until he gets some sense in his head."

Worthington shrugged but only said, "That won't be necessary."

A sigh of relief went through the crowd. It changed to disbelief then cursing when before anyone could stop him, Stancel freed the boat and leaped into it. "Worthingtons always get what they want," he called.

To Dori's horror, Stancel's legs tangled. His face changed from triumph to terror. He pitched forward in the hog trough and sprawled on his belly, head facing downstream. No sound came from his tightly clamped lips, but the appeal for help in his fear-filled eyes threatened to tear Dori's heart up by the roots.

In a twinkling, Seth raced alongside the flume and dug his boot heels into the needle-covered ground.

"God, give him strength!" Dori cried.

From his precarious position on the bank above the flume, Seth stretched out a long arm. Stancel caught Seth's wrist in a death grip and leaped to safety — but his sudden movement threw Seth off balance and into the hog trough. Before he could right himself, the boat hit an obstruction. Splinters flew. The impact hurled Seth into the flume, ten feet ahead of the boat.

"Oh Lord, forgive me." Sobbing and crying out to God to save Seth from the results of her willfulness, Dori staggered down the incline, clutching at branches and small trees. Realization hit like an avalanche: If Seth died, life would cease to have meaning for her. Her boots slipped on the needle-covered ground. She wildly tried to save herself — and failed.

The next instant, Matt's powerful grip bit into her shoulder. She stumbled and fell to her knees, hitting one on a rock. Scarcely aware of the pain, Dori's gaze riveted on the flume where Seth was fighting for his life. *Please, God, don't let Seth die. I am so sorry. Save him and I promise . . .* She could not continue.

"Stay where you are," Matt ordered before sprinting after Seth, who had been unable to launch himself back into the hog trough. Dori strained her eyes to follow Seth's progress. Her heart beat with joy when she saw that, several yards ahead, the flume leveled out slightly. The clutching water wasn't quite so swift. Matt's giant strides had taken him parallel with the boat. With a mighty bound, he managed to hurl himself into the hog trough.

A split second later, fresh horror stopped Dori's breathing. Just ahead, the flume took a sharp, downward turn. Seth's only hope was to get back into the boat before it reached that point, but he obviously was fighting a losing battle. Would the two men Dori loved more than life itself perish because of her petty desire for revenge?

When Seth hit the icy flow he knew that every ounce of stamina built up by hard work and clean living couldn't save him unless he got into the hog trough. No one could survive the battering he was receiving from the rushing water, but his attempts to reach the boat were futile.

"God, unless You intervene, I'm a goner," he cried through chattering teeth, but his words were lost in the churning water. Then a Bible promise learned in childhood brought hope to his weary mind. *"When thou passest through the waters, I will be with thee; and through the rivers, they shall not overflow thee."*

With a final burst of energy Seth grabbed the sides of the flume in a death hold, hoping he could hang on long enough for the boat to reach him. A strange calm settled over him, a sense that he was not alone. He clutched the sides of the flume. The hog trough was almost within reach, but the greedy current was too strong. Fingers numb with cold, his grip loosened. He flung his arms forward in a last attempt — and missed. This, then, was the end. *Please, God, take care of Sarah. And Dori.*

A heartbeat later, strong hands clamped on Seth's wrists like bands of iron and yanked him into the hog trough. Yet the danger was not past. Above the ever-increasing roar of untamed water, Matt bellowed in Seth's ear, "Hang on and pray."

In the twinkling of an eye, the two men in their splintered boat plunged headlong into the ever-increasing torrent.

Heartsick and trembling, Dori watched the men vanish around the bend. The sound of weeping told her she was not alone. Sarah and Katie, white-faced and clinging to one another, had reached her. Curly tore past, slipping and sliding in his downward rush beside the flume.

Sarah's fingers bit into Dori's arm. "What's happening?" she cried.

"I don't know." Dori licked her parched lips. "All we can do is wait. Curly will come back and . . ." She couldn't continue.

"I can't bear to wait." Sarah cried. She dropped to the ground and covered her face with her hands. "We have to do something to help."

Katie knelt beside Sarah and gathered her in her arms. "I'm for thinking the best way we can help is to pray, then decide what we should do."

202

"Do?" Dori asked, too numb to understand.

The Irish colleen nodded. "For sure. Should we wait here, hoping Matt and Seth will escape harm and return? Start back to the ranch?" She shook her head. "We'll know better when Curly returns. Now, let's pray."

Dori caught the black look Katie sent toward the bedraggled man who had silently joined them. "Mr. Worthington, if you don't care to pray, then begone with you."

Stancel stared for a moment, then stumbled a short distance away and sat down under a tree, leaving the three women to petition heaven on behalf of Matt and Seth.

Pain washed through Dori. *Surely they will manage to get out of the flume and come back,* her heart insisted. *Although this escapade has probably killed any chance of Seth's ever caring for me.* She pushed the thought aside. Now was no time to think of herself. Dori also tried to banish visions of the splintered hog boat and rushing water, but to no avail. As Katie said, all they could do was to wait.

Several hours later, Curly returned with a battered and bruised Seth Anderson, both riding unfamiliar horses. "The boss is down below with a wrenched ankle. He's gonna be fine, but it hurts too much for him to ride," Curly reported. "The man who lent us these horses is taking Matt to Madera so Doc Brown can give him a once-over."

"Thank God!" Sarah threw herself into her brother's arms, tears streaming.

Dori swallowed the lump of relief that sprang to her throat and turned away to hide her desire to hug Seth like Sarah was doing. Stancel's voice stopped her in her tracks. He looked more than ever like a scarecrow in his torn clothes when he shuffled over to Seth and held out an earth-stained paw.

"Much obliged, old chap. Ripping of you to lend a hand. Puts me in your debt, and all that." He cleared his throat. "I was a bit distracted there for a bit, but I could have extricated myself shortly. Of course, you couldn't know." He shrugged.

Dori wanted to hit the obtuse man. Instead, she fixed her gaze on Seth. A white line formed around his lips. He ignored Stancel's outstretched hand, clenched his fists, and stuck his face close to the braggart's. Then he let loose with both barrels.

"You just don't savvy, do you, Worthington? You deserve the licking of your life. I'd love to give it to you, but I am not going to do it. If you don't start using whatever brains God gave you, there's a lot worse ahead for you." Seth paused. "You think you could have saved your own worthless hide? Never on this green earth. You're right about one thing. You're in my debt. But you owe a far greater debt to Someone else."

A poignant light crept into Seth's eyes, a light that made Dori feel more ashamed than she had ever been in all her years of careless living.

"I risked my life to save yours, Mr. Stancel Worthington III. Jesus Christ, the Son of God, did a lot more than that. He died on a cross to save your soul. If you're any kind of man, you'd best get your nose out of the air and start admitting who's really in control. Otherwise, you're no better than the braying donkeys on the Diamond S."

Dori wanted to applaud, but Curly had the last word.

"A-men," he drawled. He clapped Stancel on the shoulder so hard the Englishman staggered. "Cheer up, old chap. If the good Lord could save a miserable cowboy sinner like me — which He did — then I reckon He can save an ornery critter like you." Curly freed his hand and scratched his head. "I'll tell the world, though, it's gonna

take some doin', even for Somebody as big
as God."

TWENTY-ONE

Stancel Worthington III was strangely silent on the long trip home. He kept to himself for much of the way, riding apart from the others in the party and only speaking when spoken to. For the first time in Dori's acquaintance, she saw uncertainty in his eyes. Had what she privately called "Seth's Sugar Pine Sermon" pricked Stancel's vanity and begun to make a difference in his life? She fervently hoped so.

"How could it not make a difference?" Dori asked herself a dozen times while riding through the forests and back down to the Diamond S. "If I live to be an old woman, I'll never forget Seth's blazing face and the words that poured out of him." A boulder-sized lump of regret rose to her throat.

"Lord, Stancel is guilty of not believing in You. I've been guilty of taking Your Son's sacrifice lightly, even though I knew better.

In Your eyes, I must be guiltier than Stancel, the scoffer."

The voice of truth that had so often risen to condemn her and been drowned out by her refusal to heed it would not be silenced.

You've flitted through life seeking pleasure like a butterfly searching for nectar. Matt and Solita's attempts to rein you in have been in vain. You've been sullen and angry with Matt without just cause. You've whined and complained and done everything but stomp your feet because your brother is making you finish your schooling: a far lighter punishment than you deserve for your behavior at Brookside.

Dori squirmed. The indignity of being made to do lessons like an unruly child still rankled. "Young ladies shouldn't be forced to study if they don't want to," she sputtered in self-defense.

The voice continued. *Young lady? Sarah and Katie and Abby are young ladies. You're nothing but a spoiled child who is determined to have her own way, no matter what the consequences are. What happened to your grandiose plan to impress Seth by helping Sarah and Solita teach the Mexican women and children to speak English? You ran at every opportunity and left the teaching to Sarah, Solita, and now Katie.*

Dori drooped in the saddle and allowed Splotches to fall behind the band of travelers. Everything the little voice said was true.

Have you forgotten so soon how God saved you from the river?

The forest around Dori faded. Memory replaced the oaks and pines with a deadly, rushing stream. She shuddered in spite of the warm day. But for the grace of God, she would be dead. How had she repaid Him? By hanging on to the desire for revenge and putting Stancel, then Seth and Matt, in terrible danger.

Never before had Dori so felt the enormity of her offenses. The crushing knowledge caused her to plead, "God, forgive me. Jesus, please be my Trailmate and Guide, as You are Matt's and Sarah's and Seth's . . ." Words failed her. Reining in Splotches, she slid to the ground and fell to her knees beneath the widespread arms of a huge oak tree. Scalding tears fell.

"Jesus, you told Peter to forgive seventy times seven. You forgave him even though he denied You three times. I've never denied You in words, but through my actions. I'm so sorry. Please, help me to start over and be what You want me to be."

Dori stayed under the tree for a long time, searching her soul for any hidden wrongdoing. When she finally remounted Splotches, an indescribable peace filled her heart. She patted the pinto's neck and whispered, "I feel pounds lighter. And clean. Clean and forgiven. Now I have to find Stancel and apologize." Dread of having to humble herself before the prim and proper Englishman filled her, but a scene from the past came to mind.

"Solita, I don't feel like saying my prayers."

"Perhaps it is because you have anger in your heart at Señor Mateo for not taking you with him to Madera."

"I don't see why I couldn't go."

"Señor Mateo had an important meeting. He had no time to watch out for you."

"Why does that make me not want to pray?"

"It is always so, querida.Prayer is our gift to God. The Bible says that before we bring gifts to Him, we must first make things right with others."

Alone on the hillside, Dori smiled. She could still remember running barefoot down the stairs and flinging herself into Matt's forgiving arms. "I sure won't fling myself into Stancel's arms, but I'll try to make amends," she told Splotches. "I humiliated him publicly, so I need to apologize the same way." She clucked to her horse and started down the long trail to find the others.

That evening around a blazing campfire, Dori waited until conversation dwindled. Then she took a deep breath, held, and released it. "Stancel, you wouldn't know it from my actions, but I became a Christian when I was a little girl. Sadly, it didn't keep me from wanting revenge for" — she faltered — "for what happened in Boston. I deliberately brought up the subject of riding the flume. Deep down, I figured you wouldn't really do it when you saw what it was like. I wanted you to back down so I could show you up in front of everyone and crow over you."

Dori curled her fingers into the palms of her hands so tightly the nails bit. "This afternoon I asked God to forgive me. I know He did. I hope to forgive myself when that awful incident stops haunting me. I need one more thing. Will you forgive me?" Dori's pulse drummed in her ears, but she never took her gaze off Stancel.

After what seemed like an eternity of shocked silence, he mumbled, "That's awfully big of you, my dear." Stancel waved a dismissive hand. "Think no more about it." He cleared his throat and gave his own offhand apology. "I may have been a bit to blame as well." Then he awkwardly got up and said, "May I speak to you privately?"

Dori's heart sank. *Oh dear, is he going to propose again?* She rose to her feet and slowly followed Stancel out of hearing distance at the far edge of the firelit circle, dismayed by what must be the final showdown between them.

Stancel cleared his throat again. "Since the matter of the flume ride is settled, it's time for you to stop this nonsense about not marrying me. We need to get on with our plans. We'll have a jolly time in Boston and go back to England often. Not, of course, until you have instruction in proper etiquette concerning castles, riding after the hounds, and all that. When you're properly trained, I will present you at court, but only after I know you are ready and won't disgrace me."

Had Stancel learned nothing during his time in the West? Dori fought the urge to laugh in his face, breathed a prayer for help, and replied, "I can't marry you. Not now. Not ever."

Stancel peered at her through the flickering light. His voice turned cold. "It's because I'm not a Christian, isn't it? If you were my wife, I might someday put aside my beliefs and become one."

Dori knew she must sound a death knell to that line of thought. "You must never become a Christian for such a reason, Stancel. Besides, it wouldn't make any difference. I don't love you. I never have. It's as simple as that."

His colorless gaze sharpened. "I say. Is there someone else?"

Dori felt herself tingle from the toes of her dusty boots to the top of her curly dark head. "You have no right to ask such a question."

"I have *every* right," he stubbornly persisted. His mouth pursed so tightly the words came out like buckshot. "Dolores, I have done you the honor of laying my heart and hand at your feet, but you continue to trifle with me. I demand to know: Do you fancy yourself in love with some blighter out here?" He grabbed her wrists. "That's it, isn't it? Who is he? One of the cowboys? Young Anderson, perhaps?"

His jeering laughter grated on Dori's nerves. She jerked free. Only one answer would get through his thick hide. "Yes," she snapped, "but you're not to say a word to anyone, you hear?"

Stancel's mouth fell open. "Surely you can't believe I will disclose your folly in choosing a California ruffian when you might become a *Worthington.*" He tucked his chin into his neck and added in the condescending tone Dori hated, "My dear girl, the day will come when you will look back to this moment. You will realize what you gave up and regret it for the rest of your life."

His arrogance loosened Dori's unruly tongue. "Don't hold your breath waiting," she muttered before she could stop herself. Then she turned and headed back to the campfire. "Well, Lord, I did it again. Will I ever learn to control my temper? On the other hand, being a Christian doesn't mean I have to stand for Stancel Worthington III's insults."

"My Son took the worst kind of abuse and didn't open His mouth in reproach."

Dori swung around and returned to where Stancel still stood in the shadows. His long arms were crossed over his chest, and a bitter look covered his face. "Mr. Worthington, once again I apologize. The Bible says all things work together for good. Perhaps this will convince you that I could never be the kind of wife you want." Pity overrode contempt and softened her voice. "Go back to Boston. Marry Gretchen and be happy." Dori summoned all the courage she possessed. "I wish you well and hope you'll remember what Seth told you at the flume." She held out her hand.

Stancel looked at Dori's hand as if it were a poisonous snake. "I shall certainly consider your suggestion — the one about Gretchen, that is." He stalked off.

Dori sighed. She'd done what she could. Now it appeared the travelers would have to put up with a fit of the sulks by the rejected suitor for the remainder of his stay.

Her prediction proved accurate. Stancel remained unapproachable during the time it took him to sufficiently recover from the cattle drive and announce that the sooner he got back to Boston the better.

On the day he left, Dori wavered between bidding him good-bye at the ranch and going to town when Matt drove him in. Still hoping for some kind of reconciliation, she decided to go.

I may as well have stayed home, she thought when the visitor refused to respond to Matt's and her efforts to rouse him on the way to Madera. Stancel gave no sign of compromising his dignity other than stiffly saying, "Thank you for your hospitality, such as it was."

Dori's heart sank. Did she dare say anything that might help the seeds of Christianity Stancel had witnessed during his stay stir his parched heart and grow? Or would speaking out do more harm than good?

Matt evidently held no such reservations. Just before Stancel stepped onto the eastbound train, Matt grasped his hand and said, "We realize this hasn't been a happy vacation for you. I hope you will overlook our brand of humor and remember what Seth told you about God and Jesus."

For a moment, Dori feared there would be no relenting. Then an unexplainable look stole into Worthington's eyes, and he gruffly said, "Tell Anderson I will think about it." He swung up the steps of the train without looking back.

Dori wanted to applaud. "Godspeed," she called to her troublesome swain, meaning it with all her heart. The train whistle sounded. Dori watched Stancel Worthington III chug out of her life, torn between tears, laughter, relief, and the desire that he would one day find salvation.

TWENTY-TWO

Two weeks later, Dori halted Splotches under a giant oak tree on a knoll above the Diamond S and slid from the saddle. Matt had ordered her to stay within sight of the ranch house when riding alone, due to rumors about unsavory-looking strangers being seen on the range. Now she sank to the ground. If she didn't let out her pent-up feelings she'd burst.

"I don't understand, Lord," she said in the direct approach that made God her trailmate, as well as her Savior. "I've repented, groveled, and apologized. I've studied until my head ached to make up for ducking out on my lessons earlier. Unless I'm sadly mistaken, I did well on my final examinations. I've helped teach the Mexican women and children, been nice to Abby when she comes to visit, and done everything Matt tells me. Yet things are worse with Seth than ever."

Splotches nickered and nudged Dori's shoulder with her nose.

"What do you know?" she asked. "You're only a horse. Sorry, girl. If I didn't have God and you to talk to, I'd be sunk. I told Solita if my life were a storybook, Seth would recognize I've turned over a new leaf — now that Stancel's gone. We'd have a grand reconciliation scene, and the book would end with us living happily ever after."

She groaned. "Know what she said?" Dori mimicked the housekeeper's voice. " 'Life isn't a storybook. This is only the end of a chapter. Dios will show you what comes next. Trust Him and wait. He knows what is best for you and Señor Seth.' "

Dori sprang to her feet. "Lord, I don't want to wait. Seth is as polite as can be but the biding-my-time look in those blue eyes is driving me crazy. Why can't he see I'm sincere?"

The autumn leaves do not change color overnight, but gradually. Seth needs time to be shown that you are not the same Dolores Sterling.

All the fight went out of Dori. Her voice of conscience was right, as usual. But what would it take to convince the man she loved that she had truly changed?

A horrid thought came. "Abby is hot on

Seth's trail. He's also mighty friendly with Katie. If she's in love with Curly, like Solita says, why was she whispering with Seth on the porch the other evening? What if God knows I'm not the best mate for Seth?"

Splotches had no answer beyond another whinny, and the little voice that sometimes plagued and at other times comforted Dori remained silent.

She swung into the saddle and turned toward home, so lost in misery that even the western sky flaunting red, orange, and purple banners failed to raise her spirits. Seeing Seth talking with Katie by the corral didn't help. He appeared to be pleading with her, but as Dori drew closer, she saw Katie shake her head and heard her say,

"Faith and mercy, has that spalpeen Curly been for getting your help to argue his cause? 'Twill do him no good." Laughter rippled. "We'll wed when I say the word, and not one minute sooner."

Dori's despair over Seth changed to joy. *One down, one to go,* she exulted. *With Katie marrying Curly, that just leaves Abby for competition.* She grinned and called, "Grand evening, isn't it?" then dismounted and led Splotches into the corral. Her heart thundered while she removed the saddle, rubbed Splotches down, turned the mare loose in the pasture, and headed for the house. Thankfully, she reached the privacy of her room without encountering anyone.

She sat down by her window and stared into the growing night. Katie had disappeared, but Seth still stood by the corral, face turned in the direction of the house. Dori's hands flew to her burning face. How could she face him — or anyone — blushing like tonight's sunset? Surely they'd see the love she'd tried so hard to hide.

Sterling pride won out over Dori's dismay. She changed from her riding clothes into a red-checked gingham dress with a white collar and cuffs and ran downstairs. The family was gathered in the sitting room as usual, along with Seth, Curly, and Solita. Conversation stopped when Dori entered. She chose a chair where her face would be in shadow and asked, "Am I interrupting something?"

"Not at all," Matt said. "In fact, we were talking about you."

Dori sat up straight. "What did I do now? I thought I'd been pretty good lately." She hated the quaver in her voice. Was Matt, as well as Seth, questioning her sincerity?

Matt's laughter boomed. "I'll let Katie tell you."

Dori took heart. It didn't sound like she

was in trouble. "Katie?"

Her teacher's eyes sparkled. "You've been for studying so hard recently that you've passed your final examinations with highest honors. Congratulations."

Dori sagged with relief, but Katie wasn't finished.

"Being here has been a blessing, one I'll be for remembering long after I'm gone."

Curly raised one eyebrow, and his eyes twinkled. "I don't think you'll be for movin' on any time soon," he drawled.

Katie turned rosy red and sent a quick look at Seth, who said, "That's for sure," and smiled at Dori.

She felt the telltale blush she hated crawl into her cheeks. Best to get away before she betrayed her feelings. She yawned. "Excuse me, folks. I think I'll turn in." She stood up and started for the staircase, but Seth's voice stopped her.

"Now that you're finished with your studies, maybe we'll have time to ride again."

Dori gulped. "I thought my lessons were over."

"Really? I may still have a few things to teach you."

The twinkle in Seth's eyes made Dori feel she'd stepped onto shaky ground. Drat. He'd always been able to see right through her. Had he caught the relief in her face that Katie wasn't a candidate for his affections? She gathered her wits and raised her head.

"Why, of course." Dori forced herself to slowly walk upstairs when she longed to run. She wanted to ride with Seth. Yet doing so meant giving herself away, and refusing would bring down a storm of questions on her hapless head. Before falling asleep, she pounded at the gates of heaven, asking for a reprieve.

If Dori had ever questioned whether God had a sense of humor, she'd have tossed the notion to the four winds the very next day. A buggy pulled up to the ranch house. Abby Sheridan stepped down.

"Howdy, everyone. I have a few days off." Abby's pretty face shone with excitement. "I'm taking the stage trip up to Big Tree Station. Anyone want to go along?"

"Where's Big Tree Station?" Sarah wanted to know.

"In the Yosemite Valley," Matt told her. "You stay overnight and the trip is quite an experience." He grinned. "Remember when we went, Dori? You couldn't believe that a tree could be big enough for a stagecoach to drive through."

"It was, though." Dori added, "I also remember the endless forests and canyons and snow-capped mountains. You'll love them, Sarah. Guess what: Even former president Ulysses S. Grant took the trip."

Sarah's eyes glowed. "It sounds like just this side of heaven."

Abby clapped her hands and giggled. "What's good enough for a president is good enough for me." She paused and dramatically added, "Besides, we may be held up."

"Held up? Does that happen often?" A little worry line creased Sarah's forehead.

"It's nothing to worry about," Abby reassured her. "Holdups are so commonplace that the tourists almost hope they will happen. The robbers are usually real gentlemen. They hold up the stage, relieve passengers of their valuables, politely thank them, and ride away without harming anyone." Abby beamed. "We'll outsmart them. We'll leave our valuables at home and enjoy being held up without losing our possessions."

Sarah laughed so hard she had to hold her sides. "It sounds wonderful and really quite safe. What do you think, Matt? Can you get away?"

He shook his head. "I wish I could, but I

have to attend a cattleman's meeting." His face brightened. "Seth can take my place, and you can chaperone, Sarah. How does that sound?" He grinned at Dori. "The trip will be a reward for your hard work."

"Thanks." Dori kept to herself the fact she saw the trip as twofold. She could gauge Seth's reaction to Abby. There also might be a chance to show Seth she wasn't the same spoiled girl she used to be.

On the appointed morning, Seth, Sarah, Dori, and Abby met at Captain Mace's Yosemite Hotel just before six o'clock. At the last minute, Katie had decided to stay at the ranch. She didn't say why, but Dori suspected it was because Curly wasn't going.

Dori shrugged and vowed to shelve her worries and enjoy what lay ahead. The day loomed bright and beautiful; the stagecoach sat ready and waiting. Dori shivered as much from excitement as from the chilly morning. She thought of Stancel Worthington III and laughed. What would he think of the open-sided stagecoach with its canopy top, horsehair-filled seats, and great wheels? He'd surely look down his nose at the other two passengers: rough-dressed ranchers who said they'd be getting off at Fresno Flats. And he'd jeer at Charley, the grizzled, loquacious driver who had Seth riding next to him.

Dori couldn't have cared less. Nothing could spoil the day. She reviewed their itinerary. Arrive and change horses at Adobe Ranch, nine miles east of Madera. Go through Dustin's Station. Stop for dinner at Coarsegold. Travel through Potter's Ridge, Fresno Flats, and Burford's Station. Reach Big Tree Station in the late afternoon.

"I can hardly wait to stay at the Wawona Hotel," Abby said when they were underway. "I heard all about it from a woman who took the trip." Peals of mirth brought an answering smile to Dori's face.

"You won't believe this. First she raved about the hotel, which is a large, two-story building with a lobby, sitting room, dining room, office, twenty-five guest rooms, lots of flowers, and wonderful food. Then she sighed and said, 'Now if it were only in San Francisco instead of way up here in the wilderness, it would be perfect.' "

"Sounds like . . . uh . . . someone Dori knows," Sarah teased.

"Enough of that, Mrs. Sterling. Pay attention to the trip."

"I am." Sarah's eyes reflected the wonder Dori felt in spite of having to keep her balance in the swaying stagecoach. A bull elk meandered across the dusty road, and Charley warned, "Be keerful of ani-mules up here. You gotta watch out if 'n you sleep on the ground floor at the *ho*-tel. Don't leave yore winders open. Coyotes 'round here have been known to sneak up an' snatch at a body's bedroll."

Seth chuckled. "Come on, Charley. That only happens in the woods, not in the hotel." He seemed more carefree than he had for weeks.

"I'm just joshin'. Yu'll be perfectly safe at Big Tree Station."

By the time they reached Coarsegold, Dori couldn't wait to get out of the jouncing stagecoach. The trip so far had surpassed expectations but she secretly wondered how much of her would be left by the time they reached Big Tree Station. Once on solid ground, Dori clicked her teeth. "Lead me to the food. At least no robbers yet."

No robbers. Something worse. When the travelers returned to the stage after dinner they discovered a new passenger.

Red Fallon was perched beside the driver.

TWENTY-THREE

Stunned, Seth Anderson stared at the gaunt man on the high seat beside Charley.

"Red Fallon!" Sarah cried.

Red doffed his worn sombrero. "Yes, ma'am. Howdy, Anderson."

Red's reply freed Seth from paralysis. Although the cowhand's formerly unkempt red hair and beard were now neatly trimmed, there was no mistaking Red's steel gray eyes.

Hatred Seth thought he had conquered rose like bile. He launched himself at the man who had nearly killed him and had kidnapped Sarah. Seth's powerful left arm grabbed Red by the vest and yanked him from the seat. He clenched his teeth and drew back his right arm to deliver a blow Red would never forget.

Red made no effort to free himself. "Go ahead. I got it comin'."

The words stopped Seth in his tracks.

"Either you come up with a good reason for being in Coarsegold, or I'll beat the living daylights out of you."

Red's face showed no trace of fear. "I'd do the same in yore place. You want my story short an' sweet?"

"As short and sweet as you can make it." Seth tightened his hold.

"After Matt an' Sheriff Meade fired me off the range, nobody else'd hire me. I always had a hankerin' to see San Francisco, so I ended up there. I got mugged and nearly beaten to death." A strange expression crept into Red's craggy face. "You'll find this hard to swaller, but it's the best thing that ever happened to me."

Seth loosened his hold and reeled back. "Are you serious?" The question cracked like a Colt .45. Was this another of Red's lies?

"Dead serious, which I woulda been if a kid, 'bout the age you were when you came west, hadn't stumbled over me in an alley back of a rescue mission." Red's steely eyes softened. "The folks there practiced what they called 'soup, soap, and salvation.' Hanged if they didn't clean me up, feed me, and tell me about a feller named Jesus."

Red heaved a great sigh. "They said Jesus died on a cross so even the worst sinners could be forgiven if they believed in Him. I thought He must be loco. Why would anyone want to die for a bunch of ornery skunks? But watchin' and listenin' to the kid and the folks who ran the mission finally got it through my thick head. God loved me, no matter how bad I'd been — and I didn't have to be like that no more."

Seth clamped his mouth shut. Low exclamations from the three young women and a loud, "Well, if that don't beat all" from Charley showed their reaction to the amazing story. Seth's skepticism remained, in spite of the light in Red's eyes. Yet God did send Jesus to save sinners. In His eyes, Red was no worse than any other unbeliever. But was Red sincere?

"Ah-huh. And you just happened to be catching the Madera-Big Tree Station stage the same day we were on it." Seth accused.

The light in Red's face increased. "Mebbe it's for a reason."

The words of an old hymn flashed across Seth's churning mind:

God moves in a mysterious way
His wonders to perform;
He plants his footsteps in the sea
And rides upon the storm.

What if Red was right? What if God had arranged for the cowhand to be in this place at this time? Seth wracked his brain, trying to figure out why. All he could come up with was that if Red had really accepted Christ, then Seth, Matt, and Sarah need never fear him again. And Seth could finally be freed from lingering anger.

Lord, I thought I turned my hatred over to You long ago. I hadn't. One sight of Red showed that. So what do I do now? Seth silently prayed.

"Wait."

The admonition pushed into his brain and lodged there. Yes, he would wait. In the meantime, "I still want to know why you're here," he told Red.

Some of the tension left Red's face. He started to hold out his hand, then evidently thought better of it. "Not by chance. The folks at the mission got word the hotel in Yosemite was lookin' for trail guides to show tourists around. I figgered if I made good there, I'd have the nerve to someday go back to Madera and show folks I'd changed. Trouble was, I needed a horse." A trace of the old Red showed when he added, "After askin' Jesus to ride along with me, I couldn't up and steal one."

Seth laughed in spite of himself, but

Charley's snort nearly drowned him out. "Not hardly. So what'd you do?"

Red's face turned somber. "The mission folks gave me train fare to Madera, but I got off at Merced, knowin' there wouldn't be no welcomin' party in Madera. I bought a sorry excuse for a horse and made out all right till last night. The ornery critter broke his hobbles and took off for parts unknown. I had to hoof it on in to Coarsegold today." He sagged back against the stagecoach.

The gray look in Red's hollow-cheeked face lent credibility to his story, but Seth still had qualms. Could a hawk really become a dove? He glanced around the circle of faces. Sarah and Abby looked convinced. Dori did not. Doubt lurked in her deep blue eyes, the same doubt Seth harbored. Again the word *wait* beat into his brain. Time alone would establish Red's credibility.

Charley's unshaven face crinkled into annoyance. "That's a mighty purty story, if it be true. I ain't a-sayin' one way or t'other, but we got no more time fer tales, tall or otherwise. Get in the coach, folks. We gotta move out if we're gonna get to Big Tree Station when we're due."

Red swung back up beside Charley. Seth was profoundly grateful. He helped the women to their seats and climbed on. The

231

two Fresno Flats-bound ranchers, who had remained inside the eating place until Charley bellowed, "All aboard," joined them.

"Do you think Red's telling the truth?" Sarah whispered, low enough so that the ranchers couldn't hear.

"I don't know." Seth stared at Red's back. "All we can do is to wait and see."

The ride from Coarsegold to Potter's Ridge proved jolting, but just before they reached Fresno Flats, the stagecoach lurched, shuddered, and stopped.

Charley climbed off the high seat and began to inspect the wheels. He swallowed what Seth suspected was a colorful oath not fit for ladies and said, "Sorry. Thet last big rut wuz a humdinger." He scratched his grizzled head with a bony finger and spat a stream of tobacco juice alongside the road. "The axle 'pears to be all right, but we cain't take chances. 'Tain't far to Fresno Flats an' a blacksmith. It's likely we c'n make it by goin' slow 'n' easy. I don't take this coach on no dang'rous mountain roads 'nless it's fit to drive."

One of the ranchers climbed out of the coach. "I'm going to walk on into town," he told Charley. "I'll tell the blacksmith you're on your way." The second rancher joined him, but Red and the Diamond S party elected to stay with the coach. "Too dusty for me," Sarah commented, and the others agreed.

By the time the coach limped into Fresno Flats and was examined and pronounced fit by the blacksmith, Charley looked disgusted enough to spit nails instead of tobacco juice. "Get a mosey on," he barked to his remaining passengers. "We got no more time to waste." Seconds later, he prodded his team into a bone-wrenching trot that threatened to shake members of the Diamond S party to pieces. They grimly clutched one another and held on.

Throughout Seth's conversation with Red, Dori had listened with all her might, trying to sort truth from fabrication. Did Seth buy Fallon's far-fetched story? Yet if it were a pack of lies, why had Red come back to a place that offered nothing but trouble for him? Had he ever even been in San Francisco? Had he really heard about Jesus and repented of the horrible life he'd led? Or was Red up to some new and devious scheme?

Dori decided to approach the knotty question the way she tackled hard school lessons. First, identify the problem. Next, weigh the evidence. Finally, come to a conclusion. *The problem? Whether Red is telling the truth. If not, why is he here? His changed appearance seems to bear out what he says. On the other hand, cutting his hair, trimming his beard, and pretending to get religion would be a surefire way to convince people he's changed. But if it's all a bluff, how could he know Seth, Sarah, Abby, and I would be on the stage today?* Dori shook her head. Based on the facts as she knew them, it was impossible to reach a conclusion.

The coach rounded a bend. Three armed, masked horsemen blocked the road.

Charley pulled the team to a sudden halt that threw his passengers forward in their seats. "What th—"

"Everyone down, and nobody reach for a gun," the man in front ordered. "Hand over your jewelry and money, and no one will get hurt."

"Sorry, boys," Seth called to the bandits after helping the girls down. "We're plumb out of valuables today." He grinned. "We heard how the stage gets held up so the ladies left their jewelry home. I've got a few dollars. Charley and Red may have a few more."

"Think we're gonna settle for chicken feed?" the man snarled. "Since you ain't got any valuables, we'll take one of your ladies. From the looks of them, someone will pay dear to get any one of them back." He guffawed, and his two followers joined in.

Dori glanced at Sarah and Abby. Their paper-white faces convinced her that these were no "gentlemen" robbers. Sarah's expression cut Dori to the heart. Sarah had been through one kidnapping. She must not be forced to endure another.

"You skunks! My brother will have you hunted down for this." Too late, Dori realized her uncontrollable tongue had once again gotten her into deep water.

"Who's your brother?" the bandit growled.

Dori considered refusing to tell him. A quick look at Sarah changed her mind. She must save Sarah at all costs — which meant the bandit must not find out she was Matt's wife. Dori raised her head and looked straight into the slits of the kerchief that covered the outlaw's face. "Matthew Sterling."

"Hey, fellers, we got us a good one." The bandit leader vaulted off his horse and forced Dori to mount. "Move, and one of my boys will put a bullet in you."

With a cry of rage, Seth lunged toward them. A second bandit spurred his horse and smashed the butt of his gun onto Seth's head. Seth dropped senseless to the ground. Sarah and Abby screamed. Dori could only pray that Seth was still alive.

"Driver, get word to the Diamond S to expect a ransom note," the leader said. "Tell Sterling if he wants to see this mouthy sister of his again, he'd better pay." He grabbed for the reins of Dori's horse. The horse reared. The bandit dropped the reins and tried to get out of the way, to no avail. The horse's shoulder sent him sprawling. His gun went off, then flew out of his hand.

The trouble the other two bandits were having with their horses showed Dori that the shot had spooked the animals. If only she could reach the gun. She flung herself out of the saddle, but her foot caught in the stirrup of her frightened horse. Dori fell, striking her head and shoulder. Pain ripped through her, but she jerked her foot free and crawled toward the gun.

Before she reached it, Dori saw Red Fallon jump from the driver's seat and leap toward her. He swung onto the horse and snatched Dori up by the back of her blouse. He threw her across the saddle and sent the horse into a full gallop. Dori's last thought before surrendering to pain was, *So Red was lying after all.* Then, merciful blackness.

TWENTY-FOUR

Seth Anderson groaned. Where was he? Why was water splashing on his face? Was he back in the river trying to save Dori?

A strong hand gripped his shoulder and shook him. "Wake up, young feller."

"Charley?" Seth's head throbbed with the granddaddy of all headaches but he managed to open his eyes. Sarah and Abby bent over him, their tears dripping onto his face. He brushed them away. "What are you doing? Trying to drown me?"

"Thank God, you're alive." Sarah buried her face on his shoulder. Seth saw relief in Abby's frightened face, but he couldn't collect his thoughts enough to figure out what was happening. He gently put Sarah aside and struggled to sit up.

The movement left him dizzy. He shook his head to clear it. Big mistake. His brain pounded like hammers on an anvil.

"Lemme have a look-see at yore noggin,"

Charley said. "That jasper gave you a mighty sharp rap."

"I'm all right." Seth jerked away when Charley touched the back of his head. "Ow!"

Charley grunted. "Not so you'd notice. You got a lump the size of a duck egg back there. Not much blood, though." He handed Seth a canteen. "Drink. Then we'll get you in the coach. We gotta go back to Fresno Flats and get the law after the bandits and Fallon. Good thing it ain't far."

Seth's memory kicked in: Red Fallon; the bandits; the holdup; the ruffian throwing Dori on a horse —

Alarm attacked with the venom of a rattlesnake. "Where's Dori?" Seth peered up the dusty road that stretched empty and menacing ahead of them.

Sarah burst into tears. "Gone."

Seth felt like he'd been kicked in the gut. "The bandits took her?"

Charley shook his head. "Naw. A gun went off, an' their horses spooked. Yore friend Fallon got away with the girl. 'Pears to me that in spite of all his fancy talkin' 'bout gettin' religion, he wuz in on the holdup. Or mebbe he decided to pick up a ransom for himself."

Seth's world turned black. Red's story had

almost convinced him of the wild cowhand's change of heart. *Lies, all lies.*

"Get in the coach, Seth," Sarah pleaded.

The horror in her eyes showed she was reliving the ordeal of being kidnapped by Red. Seth stood, but tottered and almost fell. "We can't wait for the sheriff. I'm going after Dori right now."

"No, you ain't," Charley barked. "You cain't ride one of my team — it takes two horses to haul us back to town."

Seth clenched his hands into fists and fought a fresh wave of dizziness. "I'll walk."

"No!" Sarah protested. "You're hurt worse than you think. What good will you be to Dori if you take off after her and end up passing out by the road?"

"Yore sister's right," Charley chimed in. "Shut up and get back in the coach, or I'll put another lump on yore head and throw you in."

Convinced more by the way his head spun than by Charley's threat, Seth obeyed. The short ride back to town would steady him. Charley turned the team and goaded them into a dead run. Seth leaned back against the seat and gritted his teeth at every jar of the stagecoach. The rough ride did, however, help restore his senses.

"Sarah, Abby, I'll leave you at the flats and

ride with the sheriff and his posse." Seth took his sister's hands in his. "We're going to get them. All of them. When we do, God have mercy on their souls. The law won't — and neither will I."

Sarah gave a broken cry. "If only Matt were here. What will he say when he learns we've lost his sister?"

Seth cringed. His brain told him he could have done nothing to prevent Dori's kidnapping, but his promise to Matt to take care of her flayed him. When Dori had needed him most, he'd been sprawled senseless in the road — and Red Fallon had ridden away with the girl Seth loved. If the law didn't punish Red, he would.

Seth slumped in the seat and lashed himself with regrets. *Why did I refuse to tell Dori how I feel, even after she recommitted her life to You, Lord, and the barrier between us was shattered? Now I may never have the chance. What will happen if the bandits catch up with her and Red?* Seth bit his lip until blood came. Even if Matt paid a ransom and Dori's captors released her, would she come home unharmed?

"Trust Me."

"A lot easier to say than to do," Seth mumbled, but he clung to the words every inch of the way back to Fresno Flats.

Charley drove like a madman, yet it felt like a lifetime before they reached town and found the sheriff.

The lawman hastily scared up a posse as rugged looking as he was, including the two ranchers who had been in the Madera-Big Tree Station stage.

"Don't worry," one said. "We'll get that pretty little gal back." The other nodded.

Seth felt warmed by their concern. "Thanks. I'm going to marry her if she'll have me." He felt himself redden when they guffawed, but the sheriff interrupted.

"You gonna be able to keep up, what with that bump on your head?" His keen gaze bored into Seth. "If not, stay here with the women and let us do the trailin'."

Fire ran through Seth's veins. "I can keep up. Besides, a couple of their nags are carrying double."

"That will slow them down some. Mount up, men, and let's ride. We've got fresh horses, and they don't."

It didn't take long to ride back to the scene of the holdup. Seth seethed with impatience when the sheriff insisted on stopping to examine the site. Every minute Dori was in the hands of the bandits, Red, or both, felt like a year.

"Nothing here to show what happened

'cept for some roiled up ground and a few drops of blood," the sheriff announced.

"That's where I fell," Seth told him. "Begging your pardon, Sheriff, but can we get going?"

"Shore." He swung into the saddle and led the dozen grim-faced men who formed the posse back on their pursuit. The riders remained silent for the most part, but Seth occasionally heard mutters of "catchin' the low-down thieves an' makin' short work of them," and "holdups are bad enough; abductin' innocent gals sticks in my craw."

Seth silently agreed, straining his eyes for a glimpse of the hunted men.

Time limped by. The posse didn't catch up with either the bandits or Red and Dori. Seth's hopes dwindled to a mere flicker. Despair left him feeling sick. A splitting headache made it hard to trust God. Never in his life had Seth found it so difficult, not even when Red kidnapped Sarah. Seth had been laid up at the ranch and spared from knowing she was missing until after Matt rescued her. Now fear returned with a hundred armed companions. What if they didn't find Dori before darkness fell? *Lord, how can I live through a night, wondering what may be happening to her?*

A comforting thought came to mind. "I

trained Dori well," he murmured. "If she has an opportunity to escape, she can survive." He slitted his eyes, trying to recall every detail of what had happened before he'd been struck. The bandits had flourished pistols. Had there been rifles and lariats on the horses' saddles?

"Seems like I saw both," Seth mumbled, "but I'm so used to seeing fully outfitted horses, I didn't pay any attention." His pulse quickened. "I probably would have noticed if they hadn't been there. Maybe it's wishful thinking, but it seems like outlaws would be well equipped." Seth felt his lips curl into a smile, the first since the holdup. "If Dori gets her hands on a lasso or a rifle, she can sure use it." The thought helped lift his mood.

By the time the posse reached a fork in the road, the sun sat high in the sky. A careful examination of horse tracks in the dust showed that two horses had continued on the main road; one had veered off to the left. "Looks like the bandits haven't come up with Fallon and Miss Sterling," the sheriff said. "Here's where we split up. Half of you go after the bandits." He eyed Seth. "Anderson, you and the rest come with me."

About an hour later, Seth's sharp eyes noticed something odd. He leaned over from the saddle and stared at the tracks in the trail. "Hey, Sheriff, come here, will you?"

"What is it?"

"Look." Seth pointed to the ground. Excitement mounted. "It doesn't make sense, but the tracks are turning back toward the main road to Fresno Flats."

The others crowded next to him. "You shore got good eyes, son." The sheriff scratched his forehead and looked puzzled. "It ain't what I was expectin'. What's Fallon up to, anyway?"

"The girl might be hurt from being thrown, worse than Fallon knew when he rode off with her," someone said. "Maybe he's taking her back to Fresno Flats to find a doctor. Having a dead girl on your hands is a heap more serious than kidnapping."

"Shut up, you fool," the sheriff roared with a quick glance toward Seth. "We ain't seen no blood, have we?"

Seth felt his own blood turn to ice. The pity in the lawman's eyes showed that, despite his protest, the unwelcome suggestion might be true.

"I'll wager Fallon decided to take the girl back and turn himself in," one of the ranchers put in. "He might reckon the law will go easier on him. Anderson, how do you figure it?"

All Seth could get out of his constricted throat was, "I don't."

"Well, we ain't gonna find out standin' here flappin' our gums," the sheriff growled. "Let's get going."

Seth's bones ached with weariness before the posse rounded a bend and reached the main road back to Fresno Flats. The sheriff reined in his horse.

"What th—"

Seth gave a loud cry. He kicked his horse into a gallop, heart thundering in time with the racing animal's hoofbeats and the pounding of the posse's horses behind him. He pulled his mount to a halt beside something that lay under a tree, trussed up like a roped calf: Red Fallon.

But where was Dori?

TWENTY-FIVE

The staccato beat of hooves brought Dori back to consciousness. Why was she face down in the saddle of a galloping horse? She struggled to remember, and it all came back. The holdup; the bandits; Seth being felled by a cruel blow; a gunshot; Red Fallon yanking her onto a horse.

Dori twisted her head, gazed up at Red, and opened her mouth to scream. A rough hand silenced her.

"Shhh. The bandits'll hear you. Promise not to yell if I take my hand away?"

Dori nodded. One bandit at a time was more than enough.

Red removed his hand.

"Don't you mean the other bandits?" Dori spit out in a low voice.

"I ain't one of 'em." He reined in the horse. "Let's get you in a more comfort'ble position." He stepped down from the horse and set her upright.

Too confused to attempt an escape, Dori gasped. "You kidnap me, and now you're concerned about my comfort?"

Back in the saddle with Dori in front of him Red mumbled, "It ain't that way."

"Are you going to hold me for ransom?"

Red glanced over his shoulder and sent the horse into a run. "Naw."

What scheme lay beneath Red's battered sombrero? "You won't get away with this."

"Sit still and keep quiet," Red ordered. "We'll be in a heap of trouble if those three galoots catch us. I'm tryin' to save you."

If anyone had told Dori that she'd ever choose Red Fallon over a gang of outlaws, she'd have laughed herself silly. What had changed her mind — his so-called repentance? His assurance he was trying to save her? His changed appearance? No. Satan himself could appear as an angel of light. She didn't know if she believed Red. His actions during the holdup gave lie to his claim.

"Lord, what has calmed me enough to keep from kicking, screaming, and taking my chances with the bandits?" she whispered. The answer came like a lightning bolt. Red had shown her no disrespect. The grasp on her blouse when he heaved her onto the horse had not been unkind. He'd clapped his hand over her mouth only to silence her. He'd shown consideration by changing her position to make riding easier.

When they reached a fork in the road, Red turned into the lesser traveled path. "The bandits should be too busy tryin' to outrun the law to come after us, but we can't take chances. Soon as it's safe, we'll get back on the main road." An hour later he cocked his head to one side. "Hear that?"

Dori's ears perked up. "Rushing water." Her lagging spirits lifted. A mountain stream meant relief for her parched throat and dust-covered hands and face.

When they reached the brook, Red helped Dori off the horse. Stiff and sore, she threw herself down on the bank and drank water so icy her teeth chattered. She splashed her hot face, shivered, then splashed again.

"Are you hungry?" Red reached in the saddlebags and hauled out a chunk of hard-tack.

Dori grimaced. "I had a big dinner."

"Good." Red unsaddled the horse and tossed the saddle blanket to Dori. "Rest a spell till it's safe to get back on the road. You c'n use the saddle for a pillow." He didn't wait for a reply, but watered the horse and tied him to a nearby manzanita bush. Only then did he fling himself down beside the stream and drink.

Dori kept a wary eye on Red while spreading her blanket on the ground. She hadn't expected him to care for a horse before himself. Maybe he really had changed. She dropped to the blanket and propped herself up against the saddle, determined not to close her eyes, but her weary body refused to cooperate.

A call roused her from deep sleep, "Wake up, Dori. We c'n go back to Fresno Flats now."

Dori opened her eyes and blinked.

"Sorry to wake you, but we need to get movin'." Red's gaunt face split into a grin. "You slept most an hour, plenty of time for the bandits to get ahead of us."

She sprang to her feet. "You're taking me to Fresno Flats?"

Red's grin faded. "You gotta learn to trust folks, even when it's tougher than hardtack. I hadta get you outta there while I could. Charley was tryin' to control the team, and young Anderson was bad hurt or dead."

"Don't say that. Seth can't be dead."

"Yore in love with him, ain't you?"

She couldn't answer.

"He might not be so bad off as that," Red mumbled. "It takes a heap of hurtin' to keep fellers like him down."

Dori suspected Red was trying to comfort her, but she appreciated it. "You're really trying to save me from the bandits?"

"Yeah. Even if yore brother paid a ransom, you'd still be in danger. I've knowed a lotta bad men." Pain and regret darkened his eyes. "I was one till God got hold of me."

"Why didn't you just head back to Fresno Flats with me?" Dori challenged.

Red sighed. "First off, I needed to get you away. Then I started thinkin'. If I took you back right off, who'd believe I was tryin' to save you? I figgered I had to make you b'lieve me. Do you?"

The story sounded plausible, but more than likely, Red had abducted her in hopes of collecting a ransom and then had second thoughts. What better way to guarantee escaping punishment than to play on her sympathies? "I don't know."

"Most folks won't." He sounded more resigned than fearful.

Pity battled with reason. Red's life might hang on whether she believed him and could convince Seth and Matt that Red had finally tried to do something good.

By the time he saddled up and they reached the road back to Fresno Flats, Dori's head and shoulder ached. Distrust swooped down like a bird of prey. *My*

250

thinking's too muddled to separate truth from fiction, she reflected. *All I want to do is to escape, but the only thing that may work means throwing aside modesty.* So be it. Face aflame and hoping Red would assume the obvious reason for her request, she asked in a small voice, "Can we stop here? I need to . . ."

Red fell for her ploy. He swung out of the saddle and helped her down, then walked a little way up the road. "Lots of tracks. A posse, I reckon."

She ran to the horse, uncoiled the lariat, formed a wide loop, and swung it.

Zing. The lasso dropped over Red's head and shoulders. Dori jerked the rope so hard it tightened. Red sprawled to the ground. Before he could recover his senses, she hogtied him and sprang to the horse's back. Then she headed for Fresno Flats, haunted by the look in Red's eyes that made her feel as if she had unjustly slapped a child.

Seth had ridden like a crazed man along the trail, praying to find Dori. He rounded a bend. A trussed-up man lay by the side of the road.

With a cry of rage, Seth yanked his horse to a standstill and dismounted. "Red Fallon?" he bellowed, jerking the bound man to his feet. "Did the bandits do this? Have they got Dori?"

Red grunted. "She should be in Fresno Flats by now. She roped and tied me before I could get her back to town."

"Bully for Dori. She may have roped you, but you can't expect me to believe you were bringing her back after kidnapping her."

Red's reply was lost in a rumble from the posse.

"I'm fer hangin' him here and now," one of the men called.

The sheriff leaped from his horse. "There'll be no necktie parties today. It's up to a judge and jury to take care of that. First, we go see if he's lyin' about the girl." He glared at the vengeful man. "Two of you will have to ride double. Fallon gets roped to the saddle." The man grumbled but climbed on behind another posse member.

Seth freed Red, forced him to mount, and tied his hands to the pommel. "Try to run and you won't get far," he warned.

Red gave him an inscrutable look. "I ain't runnin' no more. No one's gonna swaller it, but I took Dori to save her from the skunks who bashed yore head."

Seth's nerves twanged. "Save it for a jury." *I won't believe Dori's safe until she's in my arms,* he vowed. *When she is, I won't let her go until she says she'll marry me.* His heart thumped with anticipation.

Yet Red's apparent sincerity troubled Seth. Red's past weighed against him, but what if he was telling the truth? Hangings sickened Seth. Executing an innocent man was unthinkable. *Lord, You're the only one who knows the truth. It's all up to You.*

Leaving Fallon's fate in God's hands, Seth lost himself in dreams of his own future. He let out a yell and sent his horse into a full gallop. When he reached Fresno Flats, a crowd stood in front of the sheriff's office. Seth saw Dori, Sarah, and Abby elbow their way through the crowd and race toward him, but he had eyes only for Dori. He hurtled from the saddle and scooped her up in his arms. The look in her eyes shouted all Seth needed to know. He bent his head and kissed her upturned face.

Dori drew back, cheeks scarlet.

Seth laughed and kissed her again. "Get used to it, sweetheart. I don't aim to stop until you promise to marry me."

The roguish look Seth knew so well stole into her eyes. "You can stop right now."

Seth's jaw dropped. "You mean it?"

"I'm calling your bluff." Dori hugged Seth so tightly it left him breathless. "It took long enough for me to get you, and I don't aim to let you go."

The crowd cheered but fell silent when the *clip-clop* of horses' hooves sounded and Red and the posse halted before the sheriff's office.

Even the thrill of holding Dori close couldn't dispel the feeling of doom that clutched Seth. He had left Red's fate in God's hands, but did God need some human help? "Dori, do you believe Red was trying to rescue you?"

"I don't know," she faltered. "My head says he's guilty, even though he was respectful. My heart says he may not be."

"Same here. If you press charges, it will take a miracle to save Red."

He felt Dori tense, then she whispered, "God specializes in miracles, but I can't accuse someone who may be innocent and expect Him to save Red. What if God has put the truth in our hearts for a reason?"

Inspiration struck Seth. "We can find out by sending a telegram to the San Francisco mission. If Red truly accepted Jesus as his Trailmate, it will be safe to believe he didn't kidnap you — but there's still a chance he's in with the bandits."

Dori's face turned pearly white. She clasped her hands against Seth's vest. Hope shone in her clear blue eyes. "I hope not. I really want to believe Red."

Her words rocked Seth on his boot heels. "So do I, Dori." Amazed to discover he meant it, Seth felt the last of his bitterness die.

"Rest of the posse's comin'," Charlie announced. "They got the dirty skunks who held up my stage." An angry murmur rippled through the crowd. But Seth clenched suddenly sweaty hands. The time for truth had come.

He whipped toward Red and marveled. How could a man whose future hung on the word of holdup men and kidnappers appear so untroubled?

"Peace I leave with you, my peace I give unto you: not as the world giveth. . . . Let not your heart be troubled, neither let it be afraid."

Seth needed no confirmation from the mission workers. Sinful as Red had been, he was now cleansed, forgiven, and obviously secure in the assurance that whatever happened, God was in control.

"You, there," the sheriff roared at the outlaw leader when the band of men stopped their horses. "Is this fellow one of your gang?" His meaty hand pointed toward Red.

Seth held his breath, but Red's expression didn't change.

The bandit's face twisted in disgust. He spat into the dusty street. "Not on yore tintype. We're choosey about who we ride with."

Seth's breath came out in a loud *whoosh*. *Thank You, God.*

The sheriff wheeled. "Well, Miss Sterling? Are you pressin' charges?"

"No." Her voice rang. "I believe Red tried to save me."

"So do I," Seth said. The poignant light in Red's eyes sank into Seth's soul, but the sheriff scowled.

"I ain't sayin' what I think, but it don't matter now. Untie Fallon and let him go. Just one thing, mister. Don't come back to Fresno Flats, or I'll run you in for disturbin' the peace — my peace of mind."

Several days later, Seth and Dori rode to the promontory that overlooked the ranch. Seated on a big rock, Seth put his arm around her and spoke from a full heart. "God is so good. He rescued us from flood and outlaws, saved Red, freed me from hatred, and gave me you." He paused. "Dori, do you look forward to our riding through life together as much as I do?"

"Yes, but there's one thing. . . ."

A cold wind of disappointment blew

through Seth in spite of the warm evening. *Lord, I thought everything that separated us was in the past. I guess I was wrong.* "What is it?" he finally asked.

Dori had never looked more bewitching. Her laugh trilled out. "I can't wait to ride through life with you, Seth Anderson — but not on a log flume or in a raging river."

Seth roared. His long-ago prediction was right on target: Being married to Dori would be many things. But if they lived to be a hundred, it would never be boring.

Dear Readers,

Thank you for reading *Romance Rides the River*. Life on the Diamond S Ranch near Madera, California, in the 1880s fascinated me so much when I wrote *Romance Rides the Range* that I didn't want to leave. I also wanted to get better acquainted with Seth and Dori, who clamored to step back on the stage — in this case, stagecoach. *Romance Rides the River* was born.

As a tweenager, my favorite reading place was an enormous willow tree outside our home near a small logging town. Two sturdy branches crossed close to the trunk and made a seat. There I read Zane Grey's exciting book *The Border Legion*. A red bandana with the corners tied on top lay beside me. It held a comb, toothbrush, and extra socks. Should I be kidnapped like the heroine in my book, I was prepared with the same things Joan Randle had in her saddlebags when she was abducted.

Reading those exciting westerns and traveling through the western states with my family fostered dreams of someday writing books of my own, especially westerns. *Frontiers* and *Frontier Brides* [Barbour Publishing] are two of my best-selling collections.

I hope that seeing God at work in Seth's and Dori's lives reminded you how much He cares for us, especially in times of trouble. It did me!

Colleen

P.S. If you enjoyed *Romance Rides the Range* and *Romance Rides the River,* hang on to your bonnets and Stetsons and watch for *Romance at Rainbow's End,* final title in the trilogy.

I love to hear from my readers! You may correspond with me by writing:

Colleen L. Reece
Author Relations
PO Box 721
Uhrichsville, OH 44683

ABOUT THE AUTHOR

Colleen L. Reece was born and raised in a small western Washington logging town. She learned to read by kerosene lamplight and dreamed of someday writing a book. God has multiplied Colleen's "someday" book into more than 140 titles that have sold six million copies. Colleen was twice voted Heartsong Presents' Favorite Author and later inducted into Heartsong's Hall of Fame. Several of her books have appeared on the CBA bestseller list.